YOU'VE
TOLD
ME
BEFORE

YOU'VE TOLD ME BEFORE

JENNIFER ANNE MOSES

THE UNIVERSITY OF WISCONSIN PRESS

Publication of this book has been made possible, in part, through support from the Brittingham Trust.

The University of Wisconsin Press
728 State Street, Suite 443
Madison, Wisconsin 53706
uwpress.wisc.edu

Printed in the United States of America
This book may be available in a digital edition.

This is a work of fiction. All names, characters, and incidents are either products of the author's imagination or are used fictitiously.

Library of Congress Cataloging-in-Publication Data

Names: Moses, Jennifer Anne, author.
Title: You've told me before / Jennifer Anne Moses.
Other titles: You have told me before
Description: Madison, Wisconsin : The University of Wisconsin Press, 2025.
Identifiers: LCCN 2025002254 | ISBN 9780299354442 (paperback)
Subjects: LCSH: Jews—United States—Fiction. | LCGFT: Ethnographic fiction. | Short stories.
Classification: LCC PS3613.O7789 Y68 2025 | DDC 813/.6—dc23/eng/20250225
LC record available at https://lccn.loc.gov/2025002254

For Stuart

Contents

YOU'VE
TOLD
ME
BEFORE

You've Told Me Before

Was seventy too late to reclaim a life? Nan didn't think so. Maybe once upon a time, when Nan was under her mother's thumb, when she was trying to be a good wife, a good mother, a good daughter, she would have thought so. But not now. No way. Or, as her daughter, Carla, herself a divorcée, would say: no fucking way. Fuck that fucking shit there's no fucking way I'm going to stay with that asshole. That's what Carla said. But what did Carla know? Carla was a poet. And anyway, Nan had always thought that Carla's husband (or rather, her ex-husband), Matt, was nice.

Not that it mattered. Girls these days did what they wanted to, not what their mothers told them to do, as she herself had done, not once, but twice, or, if she were to be totally honest with herself, three times, which is where all the trouble had begun to begin with: from obeying her mother. The old witch. Why couldn't she just up and die already? It was obscene, the way the old woman just hung on and on and on, nodding off in that half trance of hers, miraculously snapping to attention whenever Nan walked into the room, which, truthfully, wasn't too often. Months and months of being only semi-cognizant, and then, wham, the second Nan walked into the room, it was: "Why don't you do something with that hair of yours?" or "Sit up straight, dear, I've always told you that poor posture is the mark of poor breeding." Half the time she couldn't even remember Nan's name, let alone the names of Nan's four children and their spouses and ex-spouses and *their* children, but she'd evidently retained enough of her original personality to find fault. Yet all the nurses and the social workers, the gerontologists and the health aides all doted on her, as if she were a puppy. "Your mother is just as sweet as can be, poor thing," they said. "We just love Betsy. Everyone does. We sure are going to miss her when she's gone." Except that, as far as Nan could tell, Betsy never would be gone. She'd already outlived her own ridiculously long-lived parents and grandparents, and now it looked like she just might hold on forever. Impossible, domineering old woman. Even now, Betsy managed to control Nan, and it wasn't the money either. Nan could use the money but she had enough of her own even if Milton, her husband, gave her a hard time, which he was sure to do if indeed she went ahead and left him, which, if she were being totally honest with herself, was what she wanted to do. Desperately. She's been married to him for forty-four years. Or was it forty-five? No: Michael, their eldest, was forty-three, which meant that she and Milton had been married forty-four. Forty-four long, miserable, bone-crushingly boring years.

Ah! But he'd been handsome. *Was* handsome. Even now, with his thick gray hair, his prominent jaw, his dark eyes. Handsome like an Italian, like some mafioso boss in the movies, almost too handsome, really, for what he was, which was, at this very moment, a retired financial advisor asleep in his favorite chair in the den, the *Wall Street Journal* open on his lap, from a family who, until they'd crossed the ocean and landed in Jersey, had produced nothing but rabbis. True, he wasn't a German Jew, like herself, but Jewish was Jewish, and after the debacle of her first, early, misfired marriage—to a German Jew like herself—Milton had seemed like a pretty good bet, quality merchandise. Even Betsy had been pleased. Correction: after the debacle of Nan's first, disastrous marriage, Betsy had been thrilled. Enraptured. Pleased beyond words. Because here Nan was, only twenty-three but already damaged goods, used property, soiled and sullied, and, what's more, leery of her own judgment, and God alone knew what kind of a future a girl like that could look forward to, even if, like Nan, she was a graduate of Mount Holyoke (English) and, like her mother had been before her, a serious looker. Why couldn't she admit it to herself, even now? She'd been a beauty, the real thing: black flashing eyes, black sleek hair, limbs as long and perfectly formed as a department store mannequin's. And so the two of them—Nan and her business-man husband, the same husband who did in fact earn a good living and provide for all of them through all the difficult years of therapy (for Nan and their youngest, James), drug rehab (for Michael and Gary both, who thank God got over it before it got to be an even big-ger problem), nutrition counseling, and psychotherapy (for Carla, who had had that awful bout with anorexia) and then more therapy, this time for just about everybody, not to mention the usual round of doc-tors and dentists, summer camps, shopping sprees, vacations, and, of course, college—had been an extraordinarily handsome couple. Of course it didn't hurt any that Nan had her own money, money that she'd inherited from her father (may he rest in peace), who'd made an absolute fortune, smack in the middle of the Depression, in the insur-ance business. Didn't even go to college but had the stuff and before too long he was a rich man with a beautiful bride from an aristocratic Southern family and a big new house they were building together smack in the middle of an apple orchard in one of the best areas of Scarsdale. But, as Carla would say, who the fuck cared about all that shit now? You've got to get on with your life, Mom.

Carla was right of course. The world had changed and no one cared anymore whether you were German Jewish or Eastern European Jewish or not Jewish at all. Boys and girls jumping into bed with each other and not caring who knew about it, let alone what each other's family background was. It was all so much ancient history. Nan herself was ancient history. Seventy. How did she get to be so old? Well, at least she still had all her parts. Had both breasts (which was more than she could say about her sister, Linda, poor thing), most of her teeth, and an intact uterus. Had full command of her wits, too, which was better than her brother, Hank, who'd truthfully been a nut from the get-go, thus rendering his increased nuttiness no more than a matter of degree, and anyway, Hank, who lived in California and had his own wife and grown children, wasn't her problem.

No, because her problem was that in addition to being responsible for a senile, imperious old lady who has been no good to anyone, including herself, for years, she was drowning in guilt—no doubt deserved—over her ongoing betrayal of Milton, and her hopes to leave him for real, and on top of everything else, she was still afraid of displeasing her mother. Only if she was going to have any life at all (any kind of happy life, after all these years of living with Milton's lumpen ordinariness), she was going to have to abandon her mother, and displease her, too. And then wouldn't she be in for a tongue-lashing of a lifetime?

On the phone, with her niece Kathy, who is poor Linda's second daughter, Nan is telling the story of her first divorce. Kathy is the family historian, and she wants—she says she wants—to get all the family stories down now, before it's too late, by which she means before Betsy dies (from your lips to God's ears!). Consequently Kathy's been visiting Betsy almost every week now, driving down in her Volvo station wagon from her big house in Connecticut to sit with Betsy for an hour or two in Betsy's overheated, overstuffed room at Evergreen, with a tape recorder and a notebook. Oral history, she calls it. She wants to record Betsy's oral history. But because Betsy isn't all right in the mind (to say the least) Kathy wants clarification. Which is why she's calling Nan. For clarification. Was it true, as her grandmother had informed her, that as a girl Betsy had been, as she had said, "the belle of the ball"? It was. Because even though Betsy couldn't remember

Nan's name, let alone the names of Nan's children and grandchildren, she was able—in addition to finding fault—to recollect the distant past, that glorious, mythical past of hers in her beloved dull little hometown in Kentucky. Southern Jews were a whole different breed and that was the truth and even now, at the age of seventy, Nan still couldn't quite imagine her mother's life of tea parties and minstrel shows and dances, there in that soggy little town on the Ohio River. No wonder she'd left. She'd had her eyes on bigger and better things. On Nan's father, for one thing, whom she'd met at a party in Louisville. Well, she'd gotten what she'd wanted, that was for sure. Gotten it and in spades, and then had enjoyed the fruits of her good luck and domineering spirit for years and years and years. Which was all good and fine. But why did she still insist that she have it all her own way? Why? Which is what Nan is trying to tell her niece, Kathy, now. Sitting in her pretty, sun-filled den, surrounded by more than forty years of family photographs, Nan is trying to tell Kathy that even though Betsy could charm the birds from the trees, as a mother she'd really not been all that nice at all. "You know," she is explaining, "the only reason I married Petey—that was the name of my first husband, Petey Weiss—was to get away from your grandmother. It was a stupid thing to do, I admit it, but what choice did I have? It wasn't like now, when girls have careers of their own. You see, Grandma Betsy wanted me to be the belle of the ball, like she had been. She really thought I should be. She wanted me to have lots and lots of boyfriends, always be the center of the crowd. And anyway, I ended up marrying Petey Weiss—" Only now she's off-track. Not that Kathy would know. Not that Kathy would know or care that the only reason she married Petey Weiss in the first place was because that wretched old witch of a woman, Kathy's beloved grandmother, had chased off Philip Ellman, who was Nan's true love, and who even now Nan was crazy about, and he was crazy about her too, which was why she'd been either taking the train to New York, or flying off to Atlanta, for God's fucking sake, to see him every chance she got, telling Milton that she was visiting the grandkids—Gary and Gary's second wife's kids—and he was so trusting that he didn't even check up on her, and Gary was so out of it, with his stupid, redneck wife and their passel of redneck children, that he could be trusted not to say anything, especially given that he and his father almost never talked anyway. That, and not her divorce from Petey Weiss more than forty-five years ago, was the point. "And anyway," she says into the phone, "the marriage, as you know, was a disaster from the start. Of course Grandma Betsy and Grandpa Ed were horrified, and rightly so, because that Petey Weiss was a horrible, nasty little man! He was! But rich. You know: we had the most elegant apartment, on Sutton Place, and every day, when Petey went off to work—he worked in the family business, which was real estate, and they were very rich—I'd open all my closets and all my drawers, and just gaze at the wedding presents. The china and the cutlery, and especially at the linens, which all had my new monogram on them. NEW. And I kept telling myself: you're a married woman now, an adult. But I didn't feel like a married woman, and every time Petey came home after work and asked me what I'd done all day or what was for dinner or anything at all, I nearly vomited. Of course I'd only married him to get back at Mother, but now I had to eat crow and go begging to Mother and your grandfather to help me out. But in those days you couldn't just file for a divorce and get it. It took years. The only place you could get a no-contest divorce was in Nevada, but in order to get it, you had to be a resident. So in the end your Grandma Betsy and I took the train out to Nevada and don't you know we lived there, together, for six weeks. In this residential hotel. It was just dreadful. Six months in this hotel filled with other young women who were just biding their time, waiting for the six months to pass until they could go to court and file for divorce. And I was the only one there with my mother."

"I know," Kathy says. "You've told me before. What about Grandmother? Did all those men really want to marry her?"

Nan has to stop a minute and think about it. "I suppose they did,"
she says.

—

That had been her first marriage: to Petey Weiss. Petey had gone
on and married a second time, too, but then his wife had died, and
he'd remarried again, and then he himself died (heart attack). Nan's
father dead, and dead for years—and such a lovely, kind, sweet man
he'd been too!—and Nan's sister, Linda, almost dead (poor thing,
how she suffers!) and all the aunts and uncles long gone, not to mention Milton's parents (who'd been, in their own cranky, just-one-
generation-off-the-boat way, sweet), and her beloved dog, a beautiful
Irish setter named Gabriel, who'd only last month been run over by an
SUV on Bankston Road. All of them were dead—the mean ones and
the kind ones, the ones who complained about their indigestion and
their constipation and their failing eyesight and the ones who went to
the club every day to play a round of golf or to gossip with old friends
over lunch, the kind who always gave you cookies and told you that
you were always welcome and the kind that ignored you or smelled
bad or were condescending or just plain mean. That whole generation gone, and now half of her own generation, too—all of them gone,
gone, gone. Except for Betsy. And if only Betsy would just give up the
ghost already, then maybe Nan could come clean and leave her old
life behind: goodbye boring old Milton with your *Wall Street Journal*
and your All-Bran cereal, your evil-smelling farts and your unimaginative and now all-but-extinct lovemaking, your spy novels and your
stupid middlebrow tastes: *Tuesdays with Morrie*—has any book, ever,
been more banal? *Les Misérables*—a tearjerker from the opening number to the last, its thudding one-two rhythms and swelling orchestra-
tion designed to dull the senses, and it wasn't even really a very good

book to begin with, French or no French. As for *Love in the Time of Cholera*, her own personal favorite—as obvious a choice as it was—he hadn't even been able to understand it.

But Philip: he was a horse of an entirely different color. He could make love for as long as they both liked, thank you very much, and not once did he climb on top of her and push her knees apart and burrow down like some kind of small furry animal. Not once did he collapse in minutes, and then say, sheepishly, "Oops, sorry, honey." Philip approached her body as if it were some kind of sacred object, first just gazing upon her, and then, very slowly, touching her—here, there, and everywhere, why it was just remarkable! Seventy years old and he still seemed to think that she was the beauty she'd been at seventeen! Not that they'd made love then, when their bodies were just aching for it and every cell in their beings pulsed with desire. No, because she'd been a good girl, and good girls simply didn't, and everyone knew that. Philip knew that, which is why he hadn't insisted, and also why, later—when they could have run off with one another and gotten married, as they'd talked about all through high school and even, in letters, during their first year away at college—he'd said no to her. Couldn't run off with Nan because he had knocked up another girl entirely, a girl who, unlike Nan, had had the sense not to be a good girl, who was in fact rather vulgar, in this smartass, scholarship-girl-from-Brooklyn kind of way. Doris. Doris Cohen, with the flaming red hair and the big white teeth, and Philip went ahead and married her, and not Nan, and when Betsy read about the marriage in the *Westchester Gazette* (because for obvious reasons the *Times* had declined to run the notice), she'd nodded her head once, sharply, and said: "Well, I guess water finds its own level." But then again, she'd been against him from the start. Went on an all-out campaign to free her daughter from what she'd viewed as a potentially dangerous affection. Actually went so far as to forbid her from seeing him! Ah! A terrible scene it

had been, too, with Nan sobbing, and Betsy, cool as always, cool and charming and authoritative, saying in her cool calm slightly Southern accent, "Darling, I know you think you love him, and I know he thinks he loves you, but you are both far too young, and anyway, I have had more experience in these matters, and I simply don't think that the boy is really quality." And then Nan had graduated from high school and gone on to Mount Holyoke, and Philip had married Doris Cohen, and though the remaining two semesters at college were nothing but a chore, she managed to graduate (with high honors, no less), and then she came home to lick her wounds in her childhood bedroom, and every passing hour felt like a rebuke, and every remark her mother had made felt like a slap, and when Petey Weiss came courting—she knew him from the club—she made herself more beautiful than ever, in silk and in linen, with red lipstick and a dab of perfume, her slim legs in stockings, her laughter a floating sultry chiming coming from deep in her throat.

"Mother, mother? It's me, your daughter, Nan. I've come to tell you goodbye." No, that wouldn't work, so she tries it another way. "I won't be seeing you for a while, I'm going on a long trip." But the old woman wouldn't buy it. She'd see right through it. Her cloudy gray eyes would uncloud, and that old steely glint would come back into them, and she'd say, "Do stop diddle-daddling around and tell me what you mean, child!"

As for Milton, she'd just have to tell him straight: "Remember that old boyfriend I had, back in high school? Yes, Philip Ellman. Well, I ran into him again, a few months ago actually. Turns out he's been divorced for years. That's right—he'd married that girl from Brooklyn, the one with the big bust. Ended up settling down South, in Atlanta, actually. Three kids, all grown. Well, anyway . . ."

Well anyway, you old boring nonentity of a walking mediocrity, you, you dull, unimaginative grunt, you obscure cuckold, you sluggish, torpid, apathetic clod, I have had enough, and the reason I have had enough, and the reason I am not going to put up with your smells and your burps and your indigestion and your manifold old-man needs anymore—and I don't care what our neurotic middle-aged children will say, they'll get over it—is that I have a chance to reclaim my life. You see, you you you you—you cod, you bonehead, you baboon—I am in love. I am really and truly in love.

Actually, he wasn't really all that bad. Just so dull. He was an investment strategist, after all. What else could she expect? For more than forty years he'd spent all day, every day, helping little old ladies and middle-managers manage their 401(k)s and money market funds. Just thinking about Milton makes her yearn, again, for Philip: yearn for him like she'd yearned for him in high school and then in college, and then again after college, when she was married to Petey and then in the early days with Milton, before she'd convinced herself that she was happy. How could she not be, with such a successful husband, with such lively, adorable children, with such a big, pretty house? She planted a perennial garden that burst into bloom every March, and over the years spread and filled out, until, now, it was glorious to behold, and all the work of her own hands. Bleeding heart. Peonies. Monkshood. Phlox. Russian sage. Artemisia. But now she needs to free herself of all that, free herself from her entire false life—the flowers, the husband, the yards and yards of English chintz that cover her windows, the early American antiques that fill her airy rooms. So desperately does she long to extricate herself from the claims of everything she's ever known that she's surprised she doesn't simply implode, melt into some puddle, some lagoon composed of pure liquidy longing on the highly polished hardwood floors. If she could, she'd set a match to the whole place, watch the whole edifice of her life burn to the ground. The material world means nothing to her. All she wants is to be reunited with Philip Ellman. When the phone rings, she runs to get it, but it's only poor Linda calling to say that because

the chemotherapy was again making her nauseous and tired and achy and miserable, she didn't think she'd be able to come to see Betsy any time soon.

—

At Evergreen, Betsy sits in the easy chair that had once been in the corner of her bedroom on Mamaroneck Road, and which has since been recovered in a pattern of bright red flowers on a yellow background, and Nan sits beside her, on the edge of the bed. She feels particularly weightless today, as if she might just blow away, or float to the ceiling, like a piece of ash escaped from a fire. She's dressed as she always dresses for these excursions to her mother's, in a simple pantsuit, with excellent leather shoes.

"Mother, it's Nan. I've come to visit you," she says.

"Now isn't that nice?" Betsy, evidently in one of her more cooperative moods, says, as the health aide, a lovely Jamaican woman named Fern, looks on, smiling and nodding, like the angel (and how could anyone who worked with doddering drooling octogenarians not be?) she is.

"I want to let you know what's going on in the family."

"Is that so?" Betsy smiles, a large, surprisingly lovely smile: she's still got all her teeth, and because Nan herself had recently hauled her to the dentist, her teeth are, for the most part, white and strong-looking. Then she says, "What did you say your name is, dear?"

"It's Nan, Mother. Nan. Your daughter."

"Ah! My daughter. Do I have a daughter?"

"Yes, Mother. You have me, and Linda, and you have a son, too, Hank. Hank lives in California." Only she is off-track, and knows it, and what's more, she doesn't exactly know how she's going to get on-track, or at least not with the angelic Fern looking on, beaming approval like a nursery school teacher. Only sending Fern out of the room isn't the best option, because if Betsy throws a fit or has to go to the bathroom or wets herself—even though she wears a diaper she doesn't like it when she wets herself—or grows fearful or anxious, Nan herself won't be able to deal with it. There are many things Nan will do and has done for her mother, but taking her into the toilet, getting her diaper off and wiping her afterward, isn't one of them.

"You're my daughter?"

"I'm your daughter, Nan."

"What did you say your name is?"

"Nan. Short for Nancy."

"Impossible! I'd never call a daughter of mine Nancy. I don't like the name Nancy."

Behind her, Fern giggles.

"Be that as it may, Mother, I am your daughter, and I want to let you know what's going on in the family."

At which point, amazingly, Betsy leans slightly forward, pulls the bifocals that she always wears off her nose, and says: "Do tell."

And out it comes, the whole long messy story: how Philip Ellman, who had long since divorced his redheaded loudmouthed Brooklyn-born wife, was in town briefly, only a few months ago, really, it was just last summer, and how he'd ended up as the guest of Nan's old friend (from committee and carpooling and group therapy and local Democratic politics days) Beth, at a dinner party Beth gave, and how the next day Beth had called Nan to tell her that Philip, who'd been seated at Beth's left, had spent the entire evening grilling her (Beth) about Nan, and how after she'd heard that, she, Nan, had dashed off a letter to him—it turned out that he'd settled in Atlanta, where he was a professor of English, specializing in Yeats, at Emory University—telling him that indeed she'd never really forgotten him, and after that, things just heated up so fast it was as if all those long years (more than fifty, but who's counting?) had simply melted away, and it was just the two of them, the two of them and their naked, pure souls, talking to each other, reaching out toward each other over the length of the long-distance telephone, and my God, Mother, she is saying, I always loved him, I loved him when I was a girl and I love him now, passion like that doesn't come to everyone but it came to me when I was young and it has returned to me through the grace of Almighty God, and Mother, why did you do what you did? Why couldn't you just have left well enough alone? Why did you drive him away from me like you did? I don't understand it, Mother, but I'm here to tell you now that I am going to leave here and marry that man, because this may be the last chance for happiness I ever get, and I just wanted you to know that, Mother, because I am.

And she's crying now, sobbing like a child, really, her tears wetting her white silk Calvin Klein blouse and falling onto her lap, and Fern is handing her Kleenex and making soothing sounds, and Betsy is snoring.

"Oh well," Nan finally says, indicating her slumbering mother with a little nod of her head. "I guess I better be going. Sorry for making such a scene."

Fern, as if in silent confirmation of all that Nan has said and felt, smiles gently, and Nan, knowing that she's somehow been reprieved, turns to leave. But just as she scoops up her handbag (another excellent thing, of heavy black leather, with gold snaps) Betsy comes awake and says, "Love."

"What dear?" Fern says.

"Love!" Betsy repeats. "Love! Love! Love! Isn't that what we're talking about. Would you like to know something, girls? I was loved. Yes I was! I was loved and loved and loved. There was this man, or maybe there were two men. Or was it three? Yes, I remember now. He was a lovely man, he was. He had the funniest hair, very thick and curly, and every time I saw him he had slicked it down. His name was Ben Berlin—isn't that a funny sort of name?—and he was the college roommate of my cousin Leon, and the two of them had come home from the university, you know, for vacation. We had a lovely dance at the clubhouse. Oh it was just lovely. All the in crowd was there, of course: Tudy, Vicky, Peaches, Jennie, Helene, and me. And the whole football team—they'd had a glorious year that year, they had—and well it was just lovely, with iced tea, and cakes, and pretty paper streamers everywhere, and of course we had a Negro band, and they were just divine! And Ben Berlin asked me to dance but you know my dance card was full full full like it always was, and I think I danced with everyone else—with Richard Rosten, who went on to become a very distinguished judge, and Edward Roth, only he died young, such a pity, and Alfred Levy, he was a lovely dancer, too, so light on his feet— he ended up moving across the river to Evansville—and well, the whole gang, really, until finally I was free to dance with Ben Berlin. And you know what he did? He kicked me right in the shin! He didn't mean to of course and he was nothing but apologies but that's just what he did! So you know what I did? I kicked him right back!" The old lady is beaming now, beaming like a schoolchild with a brand-new toy, or a young man after his first intercourse, and for the life of her, Nan envies her: she envies her for her happiness, for the wild, innocent, self-regard that has kept her afloat her entire life, and seems even now not to have abated.

"Anyway," Nan says, as if there were actually some kind of conversation going on in the room, rather than the mere exchange of scripts. Then, not knowing what else to say, she says: "I'm glad you're looking so well, Mother."

"Isn't she now?" Fern eagerly bursts in. "Isn't she pretty? And isn't she just the sweetest thing you ever have seen?"

"Am I? Am I a sweet thing?" Betsy asks.

"You know you are, darling," Fern says. "You're just the sweetest!"

"It's true," Betsy agrees. "I am Daddy's own lemon drop."

—

It's true what she'd said: Betsy had been loved, desperately so, and for most of her life, first by her doting parents back in the dreary little Southern town on the Ohio River, and then by a series of boys who had worshiped her on dance floors all across the mid-South, and finally by Nan's father (of blessed memory), who had loved her best of all, and on and on for years and years and years, until he'd had a heart attack and died when he was seventy-one, and Betsy was sixty-nine. Even now Betsy is loved—loved and petted and stroked, her diapers changed and her messes cleaned up, her toenails and fingernails regularly cut and polished, her teeth brushed, her hair washed and combed and arranged, and her dresses changed: today she wore pink silk, with a wide waistband to accommodate her girth, and a white collar. Whereas Nan herself has not been loved, or at least not sufficiently: she has been needed, and appreciated, and valued, but as for love—the kind that takes your wind away and sends electric currents through your veins, keeps you up at night and steals your sense of order—that she had had only in small bursts. Milton's idea of love was consistent with his entire view of life: that it be ordered, and comforting, and secure, and that it not ask too much, or push too much, or yearn. And all this is what Nan is thinking about as she maneuvers her Lexus through the increasingly heavy traffic on the Hutchinson River Parkway, and then stops in town to pick up fresh fish for dinner and then goes next door, to the dry cleaners, to pick up her winter coat, such that by the time she gets home she's inexplicably exhausted, and the sight of Milton's Mercedes parked in its usual spot in the garage fills her with a terrible, cutting remorse. She opens the back door and puts her things down, checks to see if the mail has come (it hasn't), and, knowing that Milton rarely bothers with the answering machine, checks her messages. There is one from Gwen Moser, saying that she has to postpone tomorrow's lunch date because her granddaughter is unexpectedly coming to visit from college, and another from her daughter, Carla, who says: "Hi, Mom. It's me. Umm. Just checking in. We're all fine. Kids are fine. Matt's been acting kind of weird lately. I'm thinking maybe I should get back together with him. Or, I don't know. Well. See ya." She knows that she should call Carla back immediately—knows, indeed, that Carla is probably sitting by the phone, if not literally then figuratively, desperate for some words of wisdom from her wise old ma whom she'd never listened to before but why quibble?—but the very idea of speaking to her almost hideously inarticulate daughter fills her, for the second time in minutes, with pain. With something that stings, something that brings tears to her eyes. How had she spawned such a slovenly, slapdash girl? Just how had that happened? All her life she herself had been so careful to use language properly, and with respect, and yet it had seemed to have made no difference whatsoever, at least as far as her children are concerned—and Carla even has the audacity (was that what it was?) to call herself a poet! The poet of the pot smokers and the save-the-whalers and the tai-chiers, or whatever it is they do out there, in that little town near Lake Tahoe where Carla and her then husband Matt had finally settled, after bouncing around from town to town, and job to job, all over the West. Settled and had two kids, Nan's grandchildren, and then divorced, because, according to Carla, Matt was an A-number-one asshole, and always was, and always would be, he controls me, Ma, you don't see it because he's nice when you're visiting but really he's just an old-fashioned sexist dressed up in new age clothing, and really all he wants is his supper on the table and his bed fluffed and his kids washed and scrubbed and tucked into their beds on time. And Nan had thought: so what? But Carla had divorced him anyway, and then started running what she called poetry-for-life workshops (though God alone knew who would sign up for such thing), while the kids were in daycare at the Unitarian church. No, she just can't call her now. She'll do it later, maybe tonight, after she's had a drink, or even tomorrow. After all, Carla's a big girl, she can wait, and anyway, Milton is calling her, bellowing really, saying over and over, "Nan!

Nan honey! Are you home? Nan! Where are you sweetheart? Nan!
Oh Na-an!"

He sits in the dark, wood-paneled gloom of the den like a bear in
his cave, his reading glasses perched halfway down his still-handsome
nose (a Roman nose, straight and prominent), wearing a sweater vest,
a pair of corduroys, and Hush Puppies, and looking for all the world
exactly like what he is: a trustworthy soul, the kind of person you'd
ask directions from, or go up to on a crowded train platform to ask
what time the train is supposed to come. This is a man who would
never so much as make a pass at any woman other than his own legally
wed wife, who would never drink too much, let alone drink and drive,
and who, when push came to shove, would come through for you. He
is steady and earnest and willing to do the right and good thing, and
he bores her to death.

"Hi, honey, how's your mother doing today?" he says. And then,
when she doesn't immediately answer, he says, "You look beat, honey.
Did she give you a hard time again?"

—

"Actually," Nan begins to say—thinking that for once in her life she'll
tell him the truth, not only about Betsy's remarkably lively performance, but also about the sorry state of her own affairs—but before
she gets to the next word, Milton says, "Because I've been thinking
about things, honey, and especially about your mother, and how difficult she's become for you, and how much you worry about her, and all
the things you do, not only for her but for all of us. For me, certainly, but
also for Carla—who called, by the way, did you get her message, I left
it on the machine for you? Can you believe it? So now she wants to get
back together with him. Poor guy. Anyway, I was thinking: what do
you say you and I take a weekend in New York, like we used to, when
the kids were little? Stay overnight, wherever you want. We can see a
couple of shows, go to the museums. Just us. What do you think?"

"What do I think?" Nan says, as startled as if he'd proposed that they open their home to a family of refugees, or move, posthaste, to a nudist colony.

"Well?"

"Let me think about it," she says, and then, swallowing hard, she returns to the foyer, dials her daughter's telephone number, and waits for her beloved and only daughter to pick up.

The Jewish Wars

The op-ed by Rachel Grossman was called "Why I Live at the JCC," and Nora, reading it to its end, felt the coffee she'd just imbibed rise in her throat, a bitter black bile. Nora hated Rachel Grossman with a passion she otherwise reserved for neo-Nazis, white supremacists, and hunters of big game. Her hatred went back, all the way back to *Yaffe* magazine, where Nora (in those days sporting long hair that swished against her back) was the fiction editor, and Rachel Grossman, fresh from Swarthmore, the latest hire. It was a small staff, just Nora, two other associate editors, the art director, a couple of editorial assistants, and the editor in chief. Grossman was the newest editorial assistant, with responsibilities ranging from answering the phones to dealing with slush. No matter. She shortly made Nora's job all but impossible. And to think! In those days—ah, yesteryear!—magazines still ran fiction. More than thirty years later it still irks Nora to remember how insistent the then-young Grossman had been to show Nora her own undergraduate work. When finally Nora had relented, it had been as expected: the work was sophomoric, uncooked, juvenile. "Sorry," she'd said. "It's just not quite." That had been putting it mildly. Two days later, Grossman's manuscript came up again, this time via the editor in chief, who told her to publish it.

Thus Grossman had triumphed—and established her modus operandi, her winning formula: the story (Nora remembers it even now) featured a smart, fat Jewish girl with an Ivy League degree working as a copyeditor at a struggling Jewish women's magazine. On the first page, the narrator's college boyfriend dumps her for a skinny blond girl on the cross-country team, and to add insult to injury, spreads it around campus that his ex-girlfriend's girth had turned him off. The story was called "Too Much to Love."

A first novel called *Way Too Much to Love* followed. Eventually there were more of the same, with fat funny protagonists working in publishing or radio or journalism triumphing over a combination of skinny bitches and dull-witted men. Then there was a blog (by then there were blogs). And packed appearances at synagogue and JCC book events. Mobs of fans composed primarily of Jewish women waiting to get their books signed. Orgiastic online pillow talk. By then of course Nora too had moved on—a doctorate in Semitic languages and literature, marriage and children, a house, a garden. And so what that Nora's own life had turned out just fine—that she'd established her own professional trajectory and managed to do so while raising children and staying married to the same man? That her days were filled with friends and books and music? That in middle age she'd established herself as a voice to be reckoned with, a cultural critic who of late was being compared to Joan Didion? That she had her own small magazine? That she'd taken up the piano and now, at sixty, could play late-career Brahms with passion and artistry? That her garden, the literal one that she'd planted behind her house in unfashionable Poughkeepsie, bloomed with great thick bursts of color from March through October? That her husband of more than three decades was kind and loyal? That the two of them still enjoyed satisfying sex?

No! No! None of it mattered. Not with shit like this:

Why I Love the JCC, by Rachel Grossman

Not only does my local Jewish Community Center provide refuge from the endless stream of perfect, size-six bodies that pervade the media, it also allows me to get away from my work. My work? I am a novelist, and thus suffer from a seemingly ceaselessly endless stream of words that flow through my imagination—whether or not I'm actively writing! It's not an easy life, being an ink-stained wordsmith. But what's worse is being devoted, as I am, to probing the very depths of the lives of real life and often full-bodied women. As a full-bodied woman myself, I know all too well how societal demands for unrealistic and indeed starvation-level standards of feminine beauty work collectively to make me feel personally judged. My own work, with its focus on realistically sized women, is an antidote to all that. And what do I get for it? Punishment!—or rather, being relegated to the back alleys of literature, where I am heaped into the "second-rate" bin called women's fiction or, even more horrifyingly sexist, beach reading. The so-called literary establishment (established mainly by men, of course) does nothing but heap derision on what it calls "women's fiction." In other words, mere froth! Alas, as the current model of literary tastes stipulates, the lives of real women and their real bodies and real concerns, as imagined on the page, is automatically not real literature. At best, it's entertainment. At worst, it's garbage. So I go to the JCC, the one place where I can catch a break from the rampant sexism and sizeism that pervades both life writ large and the written life, where I'm surrounded by real people with real, life-sized, and imperfect bodies, and can breathe again.

Had the woman never heard of Jane Austen, George Eliot, Cynthia Ozick and Lillian Hellman and Hilma Wolitzer? Dara Horn? Gluckel of Hameln? Tillie Olsen, Grace Paley, Anne Roiphie, Lynne Sharon Schwartz? Vivian Gornick? Was she out of her tone-deaf and seemingly unlettered mind?

No she wasn't. Clearly. She was, however, everything Nora had spent her entire life fighting, from babyhood up through her current perch as part-time critic and full-time editor of *Lost Languages*. That practically no one read or subscribed to *Lost Languages* was beside the point. She'd kept the spark alive, the thrill of Yiddish, the loveliness of Ladino, the poetry of Aramaic and biblical Hebrew. Versus Grossman and all she stood for: ignorance masked as cleverness, whining and victimhood posing as authenticity. A pox on it—on her broad (and outdated) Jewish jokes invariably centering on Jewish guilt and Jewish mothers, her superficial cheer, fatheaded self-regard, her conviction that Judaism was best expressed as American liberalism, and most of all, her habit of kvetching about her blubber.

Nora, who was naturally slender, rarely thought about her own weight, let alone someone else's, and she hated how Grossman consistently threw public, published hissy fits over her dress size. For Grossman, being in possession of a large body was tantamount to being the victim of a thin-centric conspiracy aimed at undermining her worth as a human being. As if there were no greater injustice.

A plague on her! May she drop dead! May she die over a heart attack brought on by obesity! If only she was obese, though, which she wasn't: the woman was merely what Nora's mother used to call "zaftig." Full-figured and curvy. Who could care?

It was winter, cold, dreary, gray. Lately Nora and her husband had been sniping about stupid things: whose turn it was to go to the grocery store, who did or did not say the last insulting or insensitive thing. One of their two cats had an infection that wouldn't clear up. She felt the icy hand of dread on her neck and hunkered down.

So it wasn't until March, when a second Grossman op-ed appeared in the *New York Times*, this one asserting that Passover wasn't about Jewish liberation as regards to the story of Exodus, but about *universal liberation theory*, topped by not one but two ancient Jewish jokes about the constipating aftermath of eating matzoh ("but I thought Moses said 'Let my people go'") that Nora had had enough. Things had progressed far beyond dreck. Grossman garbled language, making a mockery of both Yiddish and American English. As for Judaism—

for which she set herself up as spokeswoman!—what she was doing was embarrassing. Grossman's Pesach prayer, shared with readers of the *New York Times*, was:

Out of Egypt at last, out of Egypt at last, Thank Yahweh Almighty we're out of Egypt at last!

Which, from a historical point of view made no sense, and in fact made a mockery of Nasser's expulsion of the Jews, his seizing of all their assets, his secret police and midnight phone calls, and the resulting wave of Sephardi refugees longing for their lost Egyptian paradise.

To the letters column, Nora wrote:

To the Editor:
Regarding the recent opinion piece by Rachel Grossman ("A Matzoh Ball Walks into a Bar," March 20) I have one question: Does the newspaper of record have no educated Jews on its staff? That's a rhetorical question. My point is that Grossman's humorous treatment is neither humorous nor accurate. In fact, all she does is reinforce and spread falsehoods about both the practice and the history of Judaism. And her jokes are older than the pyramids.

Nora was no stranger to the letters column. Her last letter-to-the-editor, in response to the newspaper's fashion magazine, claimed that after looking at photo spreads of anorexic male models wearing pink wigs, she had become homophobic. It—like this new one—was never published.

—

But the essay that Nora wrote about Rachel Grossman's ignorance of both literature and Judaism *was* published. "Whining All the Way to the Bank" was published in *Tablet*, and it instantly ignited a war: feminists versus nonfeminists, stay-at-home mothers versus working mothers, religious versus nonreligious Jews, established critics versus bloggers, bloggers versus other bloggers. The only people who didn't seem to notice, or care, were men. Unless they were Nora's husband, Joe. Joe cared. Joe was furious.

"Are you trying to ruin your entire career?" Joe said as the hate mail on either side flooded Nora's work inbox and rained down on her from sources beyond the internet that she could only attribute to the work of golems. He stood in the door, his silver hair abuzz with static, wearing corduroy pants and an ancient blue cashmere V-neck, shaking his head with the gloom of a movie prophet.

"No."

"Then are you trying to ruin mine?"

"What? That doesn't even make sense," she said.

"Because I'm married to you. These things have a way of reverberating."

"Oh," she said, withholding speaking the "buts," which included but were not limited to the fact that she and Joe had different last names, that Joe was his own boss and therefore couldn't lose his job, and that in any case his profession wasn't linguistics or criticism or literature of any kind, but medicine, with a specialty in geriatrics. Rheumatism. Osteoarthritis. Memory loss. His waiting room was full of people who used walkers and wore hearing aids.

"Have you even considered the future of the magazine?"

She had. *Lost Languages* was her love child. It was in its pages, and in its pages alone, that the discerning and passionate lover of Yiddish and Ladino could still be smitten by the written word, intoxicated by the heft and headiness of language itself—and what those languages encoded. Namely, Jewish civilization, the Jewish soul, the world irrevocably gone and with its disappearance, irrevocably diminished. It was constantly under threat, by a shrinking audience, by cultural negligence, by the noise of the world. She ran the entire enterprise out of a barely two-room office that Vassar College had provided in the Department of Jewish Studies.

But its funding was intact. The college merely provided her with office space. The money came from a single, extremely wealthy Jewish philanthropist who lived in Washington, DC by way of some shtetl in Poland. For some reason she has yet to understand, Bernie Baer—who'd made his fortune building strip malls—had a passion for the lost tongues of his youth. He was a grand old man, who even now, in his nineties, walked to shul. She loved him.

And Joe knew that. Which is why it was particularly irksome when he brought the old man up.

"Have you even thought about how this might affect Bernie?" he said.

"What are you talking about? Bernie's an old man. He doesn't do the internet. He barely knows what the internet is. He doesn't even use email."

"But why would you risk upsetting him?"

"You're speaking in riddles. Why would Bernie be upset about my pointing out the absolutely obvious about a third-rate hack who is an embarrassment to any Jew who actually knows something about Judaism?"

He didn't answer. Then he did.

"I'm concerned," Joe said.

"So you've said."

"Because this is what you do, Nora," Joe continued. "You get obsessed about something astonishingly trite, something so unimportant, so lacking in urgency, that it defies explanation, and then, without consulting me, or Bernie, or *anyone*, you take it into your head to right things by dropping a bomb, and once the bomb detonates and the body parts are strewn all over, you refuse to take responsibility, and I'm left to clean up the mess."

"You're a doctor, Joe," she said. "And I don't know what you're talking about."

"You know exactly what I'm talking about. You put yourself in precarious situations. And then I have to defend you—even when I don't want to."

"I'm not asking you to defend me!"

"Just wait," he said.

"Wow," she said. "That's just mean."

"As if there weren't real problems in the world."

"Am aware."

"Fascism, starvation, plague, global disruption . . ."

"You forgot climate change."

"Racism, climate change, climate denial."

"There it is."

"What if Bernie cuts your funding?" he said.

"Why would you say that?"

"His wife," Joe said.

"His *wife*?"

"Judith."

"I know who his wife is, Joe."

Bernie's first two wives had died—the first in the DP camps, the second of Alzheimer's—but by the time Nora had met him, he was on his third, a widow in her early seventies who died her hair a dark brown and spoke with a weird, mid-Atlantic accent, mainly about all the important people she knew. Bernie was crazy about her. Mazel tov, a man who loved his wife.

"Naomi Grossman is her second cousin."

"How would you even know this?"

"They're first cousins once removed, actually," Joe continued.

"Even if they are—what does that have to do with anything? And anyway, why would you know this?"

"You don't remember?"

"Remember what?"

"Bernie's ninetieth birthday party."

"Of course I remember Bernie's birthday party! I'm not senile, you know!"

Bernie's birthday party had been the blowout to end all blow-outs, held at the National Art Gallery and lined with minor and less-minor Washington celebrities. Nora had been seated between a federal judge and a woman connected to the DNC. But before that, during the drinks-and-mingling part of the evening, she'd gotten herself stuck with Bernie's wife as she told an endless, pointless story about her latest trip to wherever-she'd-been.

"Judith Baer told us how she and Rachel Grossman were related. You were *there*, honey."

"I wasn't there," Nora said. "She must have told you. Not me."

"You were definitely there. We both were."

Was she? And if so, had she blinked out? She must have. A visual of the moment comes to her: she and Joe, side by side and nodding.

"Oh fuck," she said.

"You didn't hear a word she said, did you?"

"I try not to."

"That's the problem, Nora," Joe said. "You don't listen. Not to other people. Not to me. Not to anyone. And this time—" He shook his big head again, reminding her of the first pet she'd ever had, a Bernese mountain dog whose breath smelled like sour sponges. He too was named Bernie.

"Don't lecture me," she said, thinking of the first Bernie, her big smelly dog. How she'd loved him.

⁓

Bernie didn't cut off her funding, though. He merely told her to stay the course. Still, all the savor had gone out of life. As if overnight, Joe had become an aggrieved old man, filled with recriminations, towering in his righteousness, cold in and out of bed, his thinning white hair an electric halo. Worse, he'd been right—Bernie's wife was livid. Nora knew because Bernie told her. Not in so many words: that wasn't Bernie's way. "Judith's feathers are a bit ruffled, she's very loyal to her family," is how he'd put it. Bernie's secretary, Barbara, who'd been with Bernie through all three of his wives, had been more blunt: "She's on the warpath," she said. "Best keep your head down."

"How bad is it?"

"If Bernie survived the Nazi occupation of Europe, he can probably survive Judith."

But Nora knew as well as anyone what it was like to live with an emotional terrorist: her late father (may he rest in peace) had been a master of the game, finding fault and picking fights, one day heaping abuse on Nora's mother for not being sufficiently kosher, the next day for using the wrong kosher butcher, the next day for being cheap, the next day for spending too much money. And from what Nora had gleaned, Judith was a master of the form. The silent treatment, or, conversely, door slamming. The revenge trips she took, with one or another of her daughters, to France or Brazil. Once, when Nora and Joe were staying with them in Georgetown, Nora had watched while, over breakfast, Judith had pushed her chair back, thrown her napkin down, and stomped out of the house. "She gets like that," Bernie had said.

And this time she was to blame! Poor Bernie! It would almost have been better to have had her funding cut off than to know that she was the cause of Bernie Baer's torment. And after all he'd done, not just for her but for any number of Jewish welfare organizations, hospitals, ancient tumbledown shuls in need of repair—he spread his largesse far and wide. And now all this home-brewed misery, and at his age! He deserved better. Then he fell.

Nora learned of his fall the usual way, from the unflappable Barbara, who said: "Bernie took a tumble."

"What do you mean he took a tumble? Is he all right?"

"He tripped on the sidewalk on the way to synagogue. Took it full in the face."

"Good Lord!"

"Twenty-two stitches," she said. "He seems fine though. I'm only letting you know because I figured that Bernie would want me to."

"*Would* want?"

"He's zonked out on painkillers. But don't worry, he's a tough old bird. He'll outlast the sidewalk."

She worried anyway, but at least the hubbub over Nora's article in *Tablet* had died down, leaving her free to resume weeding the garden, playing her beloved Brahms, and keeping things going at *Lost Languages.* Where for over a year she and her staff (of two) had been planning a special issue devoted to the work of Esther Kreitman, better known as a lesser talent and only sister of her two towering brothers, I. B. and I. J. Singer. Poor Esther, forever in her brothers' shadows, and all three of them all but forgotten by the current crop of nonreading zombies, one of whom she'd almost run over earlier in the week, when, mid-text, he'd stepped off the curb and into the intersection without so much as looking up. The world was going to hell. But at least Bernie was out of the woods. Not that he'd ever been in the woods. Even so, at his age things happen. Nothing happened though. Bernie continued giving large hunks of money away. Joe continued grumbling, except then he too stopped. Nora got the special issue out. Afterward, there'd been a brief Kreitman revival, her books—all used—selling rapidly from online vendors of otherwise unwanted books. Nora felt for the long-forgotten author, she really did: she and Esther Kreitman, the second stringers, the unsung Singers. Except of course that Nora wasn't from a literary or even artistic family. Before he'd left them, her father had been an accountant; her mother was a dental hygienist. Nora's falling headlong into Jewish languages had been unexpected.

—

A year passed. That's when it happened. Rachel Grossman published a new novel, this one called *A Big Fat Meow*. Nora would barely have noticed, and in any case wouldn't have taken note, had Barbara not called from Bernie's office to tell her that Grossman's new novel had a character in it who resembled Nora.

"No," said Nora.

"How much do you want to hear?"

"Better get it over with."

Over the phone, Barbara read:

That day, as usual, I was late to pick up my daughter Lily at school. I'm always running late, but only because my job as editor in chief of *Uplift*, a magazine for large-breasted and generously padded women keeps me uber-busy! I'm what my own mother calls a "big girl." So sue me.

Maneuvering my ancient Volvo toward the regular spot where Lily waits for me, I was cut off by, wouldn't you know it, one of those enormous, gas-guzzling turbo-charged four-wheelers, this one driven by a woman who, at least at a cursory glance, appeared to be more skeleton than woman.

It was, of all people, Noa Miller. My heart literally leapt into my throat when I recognized her—my former professor, back at Barnard, when I was a scholarship girl there and Noa (who was then "Professor Miller") was working toward tenure—which she never got! From what I'd heard, my former professor had had the nerve to sue the university before finally slinking off to whatever backwater college she finally ended up in. But none of that mattered now, as she pulled to the curb and my heart beat faster and faster.

Noa Miller stepped out of her car. And there before me, I saw her again, exactly the same, if older: awkward, unsmiling, with perfectly coiffed hair, cut sharply at her shoulders, and now gone a bright silver, and clothes that looked like they'd been ordered from an old Sears catalog.

"Wow," said Nora when the reading was over. "I guess she doesn't much like me. She doesn't even like my hair."

"Looks like it."

"I like my hair, though." Nora did, too. it was sporty and gray and tidy, and, she thought, the cut showed off her cheekbones.

"I do too," Barbara said.

"And there's more of this shit?"

"You can read it yourself, online."

"Anywhere in particular?" Nora said.

"Amazon, Barnes and Noble, Rachel Grossman dot com."

It could have been funny, if only it was. Even so, Nora didn't go online for more, though she did wonder if Bernie's wife had had a hand in this latest public humiliation—if that's what it was, given that one way to look at it was envy. Of what, Nora couldn't say, as it was Grossman who was rich and famous. As for not-rich and not-famous Nora, she comforted herself that, with this latest Grossman novel, the messy business was over.

A *Big Fat Meow* wasn't the end of it, though, and that's because in addition to Grossman's ability to turn out new novels at an astonishingly fast clip, she also maintained a blog. On it, she freely and openly excoriated Nora's work at *Lost Languages*, calling it "a cemetery where old clichés go to die." No matter that, by their very nature, clichés were old. That's what made them clichés. God she was dumb. How had the woman ever managed to get into, let alone graduate from, Swarthmore College? No matter. The blog attacks came with a predictable silver lining in the form of a slight uptick in *Lost Languages* readership. So Nora ignored it, going about her business, and checking in with Bernie, who thank God had made a full recovery.

"Sweetheart, I was just thinking about you," is what he usually said when she called him on the phone. Either that or, "How's my favorite beautiful girl?"

Sometimes she joked with Joe that Bernie was her real father, or at least should have been. More often, she thought that Bernie was perhaps the only other person on earth who understood what she understood: that language was sacred. All language was sacred. Not only was it what separated human beings from the rest of the animal kingdom, but it was the only way that mortals could seek God. Language was what had saved her life—literally. As she'd gasped for breath and light, her heart beating ferociously within her as the chemotherapy toxins invaded her body, it had been words, written in elegant biblical Hebrew and encased in holy flame, that had pointed the way: above her bed in the hospital, there they were, floating near the windows:

The end of the matter, all having been heard: fear God, and keep His commandments; for this is the whole duty of man.

Most people hated the book of Kohelet for its warnings about the vanity of human endeavor, but she'd always loved it because everything in it was true.

—

When the news filtered out that Grossman would be appearing at the Poughkeepsie Reform Congregation, Nora predicted, nearly word for word, what Joe would say.

"I mean it," he said. "You show your face, you so much as *think* about taking a drive nearby, and it'll be over for you."

"Got it."

"Self-mortification, burning yourself at the stake, go ahead, here's the match, burn down everything you've worked for."

"Heard you the first time." It was November, cold and greasy with rain. She'd been upstairs working but had lost the thread.

"You need to promise me."

"Cross my heart and hope to die."

Two days later she dressed carefully, in black crepe with a black hat and black scarf, drove to Poughkeepsie Reform, parked at the back of the lot, and stationed herself in the shadows at the very back of the sanctuary as Grossman, in bright purple, strode onto the bimah and said: "My doctor promised to Botox my whole face but as you can see, it was just lip service."

The crowd of women roared. Tears streaked their faces, smiles contorted their cheeks, their shoulders shook with mirth.

Grossman said: "What gets my goat, or maybe I should say my scapegoat, the most?" (Pause for laughter.) "Certain women, I won't say who but maybe if you follow me on social media you'll get my drift . . . certain women who call themselves Jewish feminists not only denigrate books written by and for and about Jewish women but have the nerve to do so publicly and in a way that denigrates all women, and all female enterprise, and at a time when we women need to stick together more than ever!" A pause. "Have any of you, by any chance, heard of Harvey Weinstein?" That did it. The crowd rose as one, fists pumping in the air as they applauded their approval.

"Too bad he had to be one of ours, though," she said. "I mean, if it gets out that Jewish men can be as awful as men in general, shiksas won't want them anymore, and then *we'll* be stuck with them all over again!" Hilarity, absolute hilarity.

"I'm getting forehead wrinkles, just thinking about it. It'll make headlines."

Nora hadn't been to an event at Poughkeepsie Reform in years, but now that she was there, she remembered that she hated the building, an enormous, cavernous structure with jaggedly designed stained glass windows that stretched high above the bimah and plush stadium seating in shades of mauve. But then again, she didn't think much of the entire Reform movement. You weren't supposed to think that—a Jew, after all, is a Jew—but she did. It wasn't the style of praying that got to her, the lack of Hebrew, the washing down of Judaism's particular flavors. It was the ignorance. Not that the Orthodox were necessarily that much better, but at least they knew their way around a prayer book, were on a first-name basis with the culture. Here you couldn't even use the word shul, they didn't know what it meant. They conflated being politically liberal with being religious. Not that Nora's own religiosity was so pure—not after the shock of her father's increasingly hostile Orthodoxy capped off by his abandonment of his wife and children. That the suburban Conservative synagogue of her youth had taken pity on them had made things worse. Such *tohu v' vohu* she'd felt, boiling with a mixed-up swirl of fact and emotion, shame and rage, and furious disdain for Judaism itself until at last she'd found a way back in through literature. So her faith came more by way of Der Nister and Ibn Ezra than the Rambam? At least she knew the difference.

Grossman read:

I was aghast. There wasn't much I wouldn't put past Noa. After all, the two of us went back a long way. Even when I'd been a scholarship student at Barnard taking one of Noa's classes, Noa had had it out for me, slamming my insights, ignoring my comments, and, on one occasion, giving my midterm paper such a low grade that my scholarship had been in jeopardy. In the end, desperate, I'd had to take the matter to the dean, who, reading the D paper for herself, changed my grade to an A minus, and, shaking her head, said: "Professor Miller *really* must not like you."

Et cetera.

Joe had been right. She shouldn't have come. Nora was so overcome with her own absurdity that she nearly busted out laughing. She decided to leave but, riveted by Grossman's finale, didn't.

"And finally, I want to thank the temple for making me feel so welcome. Speaking of temples, my body is a temple. Mostly ruins . . ."

Pause for laughter. Then she told the joke about the Jew who, stranded on a desert island, builds three buildings: a house for himself, and two temples. When he's at last rescued, he tells his rescuer: "Why two temples? I'll tell you why. Because this one back there? It's where I pray. But this other pile? I wouldn't set foot in it." You'd think they'd never heard that joke before for how raucous the laughter was.

Finally, however, the novelist wrapped up for real, bowing and smiling and at last saying: "But your temple, your beautiful temple here in Poughkeepsie, is a temple I'd set foot in again and again." In response, a hush descended on the entire assembled crowd. It was in that hush that Nora was seized by a demon, a demon who sounded like her father during the worst of his rages and used her mouth and voice to make its point.

"There hasn't been a temple in Jewish life since the Romans destroyed the one in Jerusalem in the year 3830, or, for those who don't count in Hebrew time, 70 CE," Nora said, her voice ringing out in the high-ceilinged, packed sanctuary.

Silence fell. People turned around. But in the shadows, Nora was invisible. Invisibly, she fled the building. Invisibly, she flapped like a crow.

―

On the day in early spring that *Lost Languages* was nominated for a National Magazine Award, Bernie died. It was, as usual, his secretary, Barbara, who got the word through, starting with, "I'm sorry to have to tell you this," which was all she had to say, as Nora, hearing the clutched grief in Barbara's voice, knew what was coming.

The cemetery was in the suburbs. From the airport, Nora and Joe took an Uber, but the traffic on the Beltway was torturous, and by the time they arrived, the mourners, in black and gray, were already shoveling dirt on the dead man's coffin. Judith Baer, surrounded by her grown daughters, looked shriveled, as if overnight she'd swallowed a glue that pulled her flesh inward. The daughters looked tired, not just physically, but spiritually: as if life itself had abandoned them. Even the sky seemed to have gone blurry under the weight of grief. Judith Baer had decided to forgo a synagogue service. But it didn't matter. All Nora wanted was a chance to say goodbye, to throw her own pile of dirt on Bernie's casket, to hear the awful thud, the profundity of cessation.

As she and Joe drew closer, one of Judith Baer's daughters turned away from the group and stared at Nora with open hatred. Two steps later, Nora saw that the staring woman wasn't a daughter but Grossman. She wore a lustrous mink coat, and her eyes were slits. Nora glanced down, avoiding her stare. A moment later, a clot of flaky red dirt landed on her shoulder. *Literally* throwing dirt? That seemed a bit tacky even for Grossman.

But Nora was mistaken. It wasn't Grossman, but Judith who had thrown the clot of dirt. Judith was so livid she was red in the face, with puffs of steam coming out of her mouth and nose.

"Who told you to come?" she shrieked as all three of her daughters and her one first cousin once removed tried to restrain her. "What are you doing here? No one wants you!"

"Mamma, Mother, please," one of the daughters implored.

But Judith Baer was stronger than she looked, and in her rage she was majestic, and in her majesty she strode across the dead winter grass until she stood within inches of Nora, hissing: "You! It was always you! You, you, always you! With your head in the clouds, you moron, you *hur*, you *nekeyve*! You didn't even know! Oh, my poor Bernie, he didn't even tell you, did he?"

"I don't understand. He was a second father to me. What didn't he tell me?"

"You really are stupid, aren't you? It was always you, from the time he first met you it was you, but you were too young, and married—

but that didn't stop him from pining for you, you whore. What a putz! His real name, it wasn't even Bernie, it was Benesh."

"So what?" Nora said in desperation as Judith's daughters, along with the atrocious Grossman, surrounded them.

"So what? The art, the fancy parties, and the money—all that money he gave you. For your magazine. Because he said you loved him too."

But this was wrong. It made no sense. And anyway, she did love him. She loved him still. She always would.

"He said the magazine made his heart happy," Nora managed to say.

"He couldn't have cared less about the magazine. When it came to business, he was a genius, a gold mine! But books, words, poetry? He was practically illiterate in five languages!"

Now Nora was so confused she didn't know if Judith was playing some sick prank on her or had merely lost her mind. "But the books, the articles—" she said. "Bernie and I argued over which of Saul Bellow's novels was the best, and whether Malamud was too derivative of Peretz."

At that, Judith Baer's expression turned from rage to raw incomprehension.

"The books? I read them aloud to him. Yiddish he could read okay. English gave him trouble."

With Judith Baer's face nearly pressed to hers, Nora could see its thousands of wrinkles, its paperlike translucence, and hear, as if for the first time, that her strange, slightly British inflections were undergirded by the gutturals and glottals of Brooklyn or Queens.

"Makhasheyfe!" she said. "Dummkopf! Fey, fey, fey!"

Clearly, it was time to turn around and leave. Joe, who had taken her arm and was gently tugging her, knew it. The daughters knew it. No doubt Grossman did too. As for Judith Baer—she couldn't have been any clearer. But Nora couldn't bear not saying a proper goodbye to the one man who had really and truly loved her, the sole human being who had really and truly wanted her to shine. A single clot of earth, and then she'd leave. She tried to make a break for it, but in her desperation the toe of her shoe caught on a clump of sod, and she tumbled, face-first and flailing, a thousand moments of hurtling toward the earth, until she landed safely in Rachel Grossman's outstretched arms.

Angels of the Lake

Six women died during that one year, all but one of cancer, and that one, Shelley Saltz, had had cancer years before. It was strange, five women, all with mailboxes jauntily announcing their family's presence on the North Road, houses that dotted the shore of the lake, summers spent picking wild blueberries and baking them into pies and pancakes, first with children and then with grandchildren and then, as chemo and nausea and bone loss took hold, not at all.

The brightly colored mailboxes (Nedra Frye had personally painted hers yellow with uneven pink polka dots) remained, as did the houses on the shore, the sailboats, the battered canoes, the smell of rain, the collections of pinecones and children's drawings, but most of all— it goes without saying—what remained were the husbands. It took no one by surprise when, just a year after Ellen Trowbridge had died (ovarian cancer), her widower, Calvin, showed up in the wedding pages of the *New York Times* with a woman he'd apparently known for better than thirty years, though, according to the text that accompanied a photograph of a beaming, bald Calvin with his clearly crinkled and sun-dried bride, the two of them had never lived in the same city. The last of the families to have "discovered" (as the summer people said), the beauty and quiet loveliness of Lake Lantern, the Trowbridges were considered to be somewhat on the flashy side, always improving

41

their property, which wasn't modest to begin with. Hardly: where once a three-bedroom wood-shingled cottage had stood, there now loomed three large and handsome houses with enormous plate glass windows gazing west, as if posing for the cameras, with the lake lying majestically beneath. Just three years earlier, with Ellen bloated and shaking from endless treatments and talking about who she wanted to speak at her funeral, Calvin had put in a tennis court. Now he and his new wife—a Frenchwoman by birth who'd kept her name—could be seen batting the tennis ball around at all hours, sometimes to each other, other times in the company of other couples. It wasn't a problem: people were happy for Calvin. He'd been devoted to Ellen during the long years of her illness. Why shouldn't he remarry, and if his new wife was younger than he was, what of it? At sixty-something, she was hardly a baby herself. And God alone knew that Calvin deserved a little happiness, a little fun, before his own old age encroached, and the new wife (Susan? Suzanne?) was a sunny, friendly, sporty sort of person, happy to tell you about her own first marriage to an American she'd met during a college trip to the States, her childhood riding ponies in Normandy, and how in the end she knew she could never leave New York, where she and her first husband, a hospital administrator, had lived. "After forty years here, I am a New Yorker, no?" she said in her lovely accent. Calvin introduced her as "my beautiful wife."

Within a year of Calvin's marriage, Peter Saltz, Eric Zamboni, and Stu Levine had also shown up at various lake gatherings—the Fourth of July parade, the annual Football-Fun-Fundraiser for the high school (summer people versus year-rounders), the 5k race for the fire department—with women of the more-or-less permanent-status sort: a retired schoolteacher with faded brown hair and freckled arms; a woman who owned an art gallery on Beacon Street; and, for Stu Levine, his grown children's former Hebrew tutor, an Israeli who'd lived in Washington, DC (where Stu still practiced law) for most of her adult life, connected first to the embassy and then to the man who became her husband before disappearing, himself, into the jaw and maw of illness and death. What could you do, the remaining intact, somewhat younger couples, asked themselves. No one was getting any younger and in the end . . . well, in the end, there was only one end, for all of them. The question wasn't how you were going to face your own death, or when you were going to die, but rather, how to live life as the remaining half of a marriage. Was there something in the water, they jokingly asked, thinking of those five women, all of them dead within the same one year. But the thought was quickly dismissed: the waters, if anything, were an elixir, a magical sweet pool of such fragrant clarity that plunging into it revived one's early sense of wonder. Still . . . it happened, and regularly: husbands left alone, without their wives, wives left without their husbands. What if? What if? Most of the women were quick to declare that, if they predeceased their own husbands, they'd hope and expect their husbands to remarry and the sooner the better. They said things like: "You? Live alone? For how long—a week?" And: "Honey, you still can't so much as locate the washing machine. What would you do? Invest in an endless supply of underwear?" The forty- and fifty- and even sixty-something husbands were not, as a rule, as jocose as their wives, not so generous with their futures. They crossed their arms and said things like: "I wouldn't want you to be alone, either, but I also wouldn't want you to rush into anything."

The widower who held out the longest, and in fact didn't seem inclined to remarry at all, was Donald Frye, which took everyone by surprise, because Donald Frye had been devoted, practically to the point of adoration, to Nedra. They'd had the kind of marriage that other people talk about in tones of wonder and envy. How did they do it? Never a cross word, never a dismissive glance, not so much as an impatient sigh ever passed between them. He'd stayed with her in the hospital, night after night, after her initial surgery, fixed her favorite foods and tempted her with homemade puddings and soups when her appetite was poor; and of course, it had been Donald, rather than a hired aide or someone from hospice, who'd nursed her through her final illness, staying with her as her breathing became labored, and then shallow, and then indefinite, and then no more. He was devastated, of course. Lost weight. Moped around. Took long walks with the dogs. People said that he was going under, that his mourning was taking too long, and was too severe. Was it good for him to be on the lake all alone—all alone in that house filled with family memorabilia and Nedra's faded sundresses? Then his grown daughters and their children and old friends started to visit, filling the ramshackle cottage with bustle and the smells of cooking, and bit by bit he resumed doing the things he loved to do. Once again he was seen paddling his canoe across the lake with one or the other of his mutts sitting in the hull; once more he showed up at picnics talking about books—he and Nedra, both, had been great readers—or the heron he'd seen fly over the cove. The worst of his grief behind him, it seemed obvious that he should, and would, marry again, particularly as, more than anyone else that anyone could think of, Donald Frye was exactly the kind of man—loving, dedicated, kind, generous—who would *want* to marry again. They'd been happy, Donald and Nedra, she with her bright colors and box of paints, he with his wistful longing for the freedom and grace of nature. He *knew* how to be married. He was a handsome man too, with beautiful curling silver hair and blue eyes. Women noticed and liked him. Why should he hold back? What was stopping him?

Even Tommy Tompkins remarried. Two and a half years after Calvin Trowbridge's photo appeared in the wedding pages of the *New York Times* with his French bride, Tommy Tompkins was spotted on the lake in a new speedboat, a white-blond woman in a red dress by his side. Moreover, the woman—whose name, it was soon found out, was Ray—was appropriate in every way, a widow herself, and a grandmother several times over. Everyone was delighted for him, of course, but surprised, too, because Tommy Tompkins hadn't been very good to Debbie Tompkins, either before or after she'd been found to have an inoperable tumor in her left lung (and the irony, of course, was that she'd quit smoking years earlier), and it had always struck everyone that the man had never been made for marriage to begin with. With Debbie he'd been impatient, dismissive of her opinions, easily annoyed. Every now and again, when she said something that he found particularly irksome, he'd roll his eyes. If she made an offhand remark about trouble in the Middle East or the rising cost of housing, he'd say, "Deb gets all her ideas verbatim from NPR," or "My wife, the commentator." It was embarrassing, but Debbie didn't seem to mind, or rather, if she did mind (as people suspected) she'd long since learned to hide her feelings. But that wasn't the worst of Tommy's sins in the marital department. There were stories that went around about him: and though stories were only stories, certain townspeople—Doug Smolers, for one—had seen him, always in the offseason, with a woman with long dark hair and big dark glasses. Doug owned both the Tire King and the gas station, so he tended to know what was what. Moreover, he was no gossip. But one night at dinner he mentioned what he'd seen to his wife, Lu, saying, "I don't know what to think. It being the offseason and all. And they never come up here past October." Lu just looked at him, shrugging. But she couldn't resist. She cleaned half the summerhouses on the lake. She wasn't surprised, she told her various employers as she vacuumed and mopped the following June. Tommy? He was that kind of man. There were men like him everywhere: afraid of death, they were, afraid of the natural aging process, afraid to let go. And it didn't hurt that Tommy was wealthy, though where exactly his wealth came from no one knew, but then again, none of the summer people were exactly impoverished. The only one who seemed to worry about money was Eric Zamboni, even though he'd managed to sell his real estate brokerage in Delaware for a tidy profit before retiring and spending all his summers on the lake, where he remained a modest, quiet sort of man, happily puttering around the low-lying, drafty three-bedroom cottage that, at one point, had been the dining hall of a girls' camp. When he finally married his retired schoolteacher, in late August a full three years after she'd started showing up at the lake and insisting that the only way to make a real mint julep was with real mint, preferably of the homegrown variety, he did nothing in the way of home improvement other than change the name on the mailbox, and his bride—Mary—didn't seem to mind in the least.

So that was that: all of them married, all to more-or-less reasonably aged and faded women, many of them widows themselves, with grown children and grandchildren and a high delight to find that, for them, there was a second act after all. All but Donald Frye, that is. It was three years, then four, then five, and Donald didn't seem the slightest bit interested in finding someone to spend his remaining years with. When you asked him how he was, he'd always look slightly distracted, as if he didn't recognize you, but then he'd snap out of it and, smiling, say, "I'm still here, aren't I?"

"Maybe he feels that there will never be another woman he can love as much as he loved Nedra," you'd hear.

"Maybe he just isn't interested."

"Maybe he's content with his grandchildren and his bird-watching."

"Not everyone feels the need to remarry."

"Or he just hasn't met the right one."

But such explanations, offered at cookouts and birthday parties, weren't satisfying, and in any event, Donald was rarely alone. In fact, after the first quiet years of tightly held pain, Donald's social life swung into high gear. The first few women he brought to the lake were young—far younger than he was, in their late forties and early fifties, the same ages as his own three daughters. At first, they seemed carbon copies of one another, with bad divorces behind them, and an uncertain financial future, but then a pattern began to emerge, with each succeeding too young woman becoming more stable and robust, more independent and hopeful, than the one before. Thus a struggling artist was replaced by a physical therapist who in turn was replaced by a college professor (anthropology) who gave way to a woman who owned a stable in northwest Connecticut who finally succumbed to an investment banker who herself disappeared in the wake of a pediatrician. It was hard to really keep track—though God knows we tried—because sometimes the woman would only last for a single weekend, sometimes as little as a single overnight. "Got to hand it to him," people said.

"At least he's not moping around, thinking about Nedra."

"Behold what Viagra has wrought."

"May he live and be happy."

"His daughters couldn't be too thrilled."

"It's his September song."

Among the women there were questions of sex itself: how much and how often? How long did it last and how inventive was it? How important was it, at a certain age? Was it accomplished in the usual way? Or had it been replaced, by and large, by something approximating snuggling?

We wanted to know, we were curious and eager, because we ourselves, the no-longer-young-ones, had floppy stomachs and soft upper arms and streaks of gray in our hair. What once had been spontaneous and natural and easy no longer was, and we wondered at ourselves, and at our husbands, and children, and especially, when we were washing dishes or pulling laundry in off the line (something we all did on the lake, though God knows we wouldn't have dreamed of putting up drying lines in our backyards in the suburbs), at our neighbors. We were either the recently arrived, with money made on Wall Street, or the long-grown children of parents who had bought the old camp cottages and tumbledown guesthouses and converted

them to summerhouses when we were tiny and lake property went
for a song—it was we who had been raised on stories about how,
once upon a time, the entire region was dotted with summer camps,
where our parents had spent their own summers playing tennis and
learning how to canoe, only now... who can afford it? And even
if you could, there were all those other, competing activities for
youngsters, summers in Europe or trekking through the Andes, and
the days of eating s'mores around the campfire and Color War were
over. But the place—the place itself, with its wonderful clean aromas... pine, Queen Anne's lace, rain... and miraculously clear water
—remained. "Aren't we the lucky ones?" our parents would tell us.
And we were.

    Then the women Donald invited up became even younger—
thirtyish and never-before-married, or thirty-six, with a baby in tow.
And there were young men, too, graduate student types, struggling
playwrights, wistful save-the-worlders, spending weeks at a time at
the Fryes' boxy house on a spit of land that divided the long west-
ern half of the lake from the shorter, wider eastern part. Were the
women friends of his daughters? It seemed unlikely. Were the men
gay? What was Donald up to as he rounded the corner into his eight-
ies, his hair as silver and thick as ever, his eyes as blue? Unlike most of
the other widowers on the lake, he'd never retired, but rather, taken
sabbaticals to care for his ailing wife. Now his name, and the name of
his company, began to appear in the pages of the Boston papers. It was
a small investment bank, people said. Or not. It was a holding company. It was a brokerage house. It was none of these things, but rather,
an export-import business, something to do with orange juice pulp.
Donald flew to Argentina. He flew to China. He flew to Vietnam. He
had gotten into the cell phone business. He was expanding computer
services in the former Eastern Bloc. But when you asked him—and
we did—he demurred. "Business is boring," he'd say. "Let's talk about
something else. Reading anything good?"

There was no more to do at the Fryes' house than at anyone else's (unless of course you counted the sprawling—some said ostentatious—Trowbridge place, with its tennis court and speedboat), but perhaps, like Nedra, the young men and women who came to visit amused themselves by taking long soulful walks, or collecting pinecones and wild daisies, or by reading. The Frye house had a real library, everything from Sherlock Holmes to Beowulf to the latest Stephen King. Once, years earlier, when she was still feeling well enough to take jaunts into town, Nedra had come back from the annual library sale with the complete works of Shakespeare, bound in faded red, with commentary by some Oxford don. Perhaps they were in there reading *A Midsummer Night's Dream*. The one thing that was certain was that one of them got out Nedra's box of paints and repainted the mailbox, covering it with twisting vines and butterflies, all deep greens and soft purplish blue.

Nedra had been a beautiful woman—even in her last illness, she was beautiful, with incredible high cheekbones and a wide mouth and dimples—but the thirtyish friends (companions? lovers?) of Donald were, on the whole, unremarkable. On the other hand, they were young: there were women in scant bathing suits, appearing in public in miniskirts and tight pants. The men often went around in nothing more than a pair of shorts, their feet thrust into sandals. Sometimes they accompanied Donald on the long walks he took with his bird-watching binoculars. Donald's own daughters, in the meantime, came around less and less often. I'd grown up with them—summer after summer on the lake. I missed seeing them, hearing about their adult lives and watching their children grow up. But Donald didn't seem to mind.

The people who minded were the other husbands—not the widowers, who, as a group, seemed wonderfully content with their second wives (even the smarmy Tommy Tompkins appeared at social gatherings visibly delighted by his second wife, Ray, who'd long since let her white-blond hair go white-gray, and who told stories about her grand-children's exploits). Rather, it was the younger set, the now middle-aged children of the first homeowners, their sons and sons-in-law, who looked at us, at their wives of many years, and saw heartbreak. They turned toward us and saw what they'd always seen—contentment and comfort and understanding, trust and love and a long history of working things out—and then they looked toward Donald Frye's boxy house set back from the rocks by a strip of grass and blueberry bushes and ungrown evergreen underbrush, and they knew that there was—there had to be—more.

Betsy Yates's husband actually had an affair, but it was stupid—he took up with an extravagantly dressed local woman who suffered from anxiety attacks and had two ex-husbands—and it petered out almost before it began, with the usual trips to the marriage counselor and the gym to patch things over. Joanna Anthony's husband became terribly depressed and ended up losing thirty pounds before finally declaring that he was sick and tired of being a lawyer and really just wanted to teach piano, which meant that Joanna herself had to go back to work as a landscape architect, which wasn't something she really wanted to do again, at least not full-time. Lil Hutchinson's husband sold his orthodontics practice and went back to school to study comparative religion. One of Donald Frye's own sons-in-law, the British diplomat who'd married my friend Beth (and weren't the rest of us girls on the lake envious of Beth for her debonair husband with his clipped BBC speech and elegant bearing?), announced that he had fallen in love with a staff lawyer at the justice department, packed his bags, and left his wife, stunned and startled and utterly undone, in their modern house in the Virginia suburbs.

As for me: slowly at first and then not-so-slowly, Charlie lost interest. When I asked him what was going on, when I prodded him for his thoughts, for his moods, when I suggested that we were going through changes together, and that change was the essence and very timbre of life, he'd just gaze at the floor, or at his feet resting on the floor, or sometimes at the carpet. Our own children (a boy and a girl) were both in college; our own dog, Larry, was creeping around on arthritic legs; our marriage had had its ups and downs. And yet—and yet! We laughed at the same jokes, enjoyed the same movies, bought tribal rugs and used crockery together. And, too, there was sex—not as often, or as passionate, as it had been, once—before children— before illness—before worries—before, before. I looked to the mirror and knew I saw what my own mother, and her mother before her, saw: a woman whose beauty and charm was gone.

—

Six summers after Nedra Frye died, her husband holding her hand, Donald Frye's house remained shuttered. It wasn't just that he no longer filled its rooms with men and women in the full flush and strength of not-yet-middle-aged adulthood, but, somewhat shockingly, he didn't come as well. He didn't come in June, he didn't come in July, and by the time August rolled around, people were saying that he'd put the house on the market, and it was all very hush-hush, as he didn't want anyone—even his daughters—to know that he was unloading it. Where *were* the daughters, for that matter? Our summers had been entangled well into college, when all four of us finally spun out and away—me to graduate school (in art history) and then to London (for my postdoc) and finally back home, to a job at a museum in Connecticut and a husband who on our first date said that he wanted at least three children, and the Frye girls to their own futures, in Los Angeles and Nashville and Washington, DC.

"Three children?" I'd said, terrified, as I gazed into my future husband's lean, intelligent face.

"Or four. Five. Two. As long as we have them."

One night, after our children (busy with their own lives) had come and gone, my husband turned to me in bed and said: "Put down your book." I was rereading *The Brothers Karamazov*, amazed by how much of it I'd forgotten. Taking the book from me, he rolled over onto his side. I thought he was going to embrace me in a prelude to love-making. He was wearing striped pajamas with a button missing where his ribs met his belly in an inverted V. I was wearing an old, oversized T-shirt. The house we were in had once been the gatekeeper's house at a summer lodge. My parents had bought it in 1960, just before I was born, adding a modern kitchen that was no longer modern, a bath-room, and an outdoor shower. They'd stopped coming up the same year that Mother had gone into assisted living, in Baltimore, though when I talked to her—to them—on the phone, begging them to make the trip, telling them that I would fetch them myself, that I'd rent a big comfortable car for the journey—they always promised they would think about it. There was rain rolling in from the west. You could hear it coming in from New Hampshire, how it held to the tops of the mountains. I was suddenly gripped by a great and terrible desire to go to Paris and see the Picassos there, a desire like a seizure, like a shower of electricity in my brain.

"Jules," he said—his pet name for me, of course, as professionally I am always "Julia": Dr. Julia Sanders. "Jules" itself was just a precursor for the more playful pet names: "Jewel," "Rubies," "Pearl."

"Charlie," I answered back. He stretched, arching his back so his chest nestled closer to my shoulder.

Could I? Would I? After the seasons of uninterest, I wasn't sure I could summon the old desire, though perhaps, I thought, I could whip something up—engaging in some spurious dirty fantasies, some of the more salacious movies and TV shows I'd recently seen.

"It's just," he said, "that I don't quite know what to do anymore. Not professionally so much. I like my work—my career is in good shape." Charlie was a contractor, with his own design-and-build firm. His clients tended to want the natural look, restoring their crumbling nineteenth-century multifamily homes to their original gambrel-roofed majesty, with new wraparound porches, or slate-and-copper roofing. Our interests—mine in art, his in design—dovetailed. We'd always understood each other. That was the beauty of it.

"What do you mean?" I said.

"It's not the kids either, though, I don't know. I miss having them around. I don't feel old enough to have kids who don't need me anymore."

"They still need you."

"To pay their tuition," he said. "And it's not you, either. It's me. I know it's me but I don't know what it is about me that's the problem. It's almost, I don't know."

"What?"

"Do you ever think that we—you and I—didn't so much as make a profound mistake, but rather, that we're still pretending, still acting, almost, as if we were in a play, as if we knew what we're doing but really are merely hurtling along, *faking it*, putting on the face of husband and wife, of father and mother, of professionals—the mortgage, the kids in college, your vegetable garden, all of it—when really it's just sort of, I don't know, *thin*. Like we're merely skating on the surface of life, thinking that the ice *is* life, but really, the real stuff, the real life, is the pond beneath, all that dark water."

"Where it's cold. Where, if you fell in, you'd probably drown."

"Or maybe not. Maybe you'd just be shocked by the cold. Maybe you'd just know something you didn't know before."

"Or maybe you'd die."

"Maybe," he said. Then he said: "Do you remember that girl I dated in college, Jessica?"

"What about her?"

"I read in the alum magazine that she'd adopted a child from China."

"Isn't she kind of old to become a mommy?"

"I guess not."

"Okay," I said, sitting up a little in the dim dark light. "So she adopted a child from China. This leads you to conclude what exactly?"

"I don't know," my husband said. "It just got me thinking, is all."

Of course I remembered Jessica—not that I'd ever met her. She'd been mean to my husband during their college romance, and he'd been obsessed with her. She ended up marrying and divorcing a real estate developer in Atlantic City, and then remarrying, this time to an older man who with a huge income from the investments that his own father, a sharp and hungry Irishman, had made just before the Second World War. I knew all this because, on occasion, Charlie would tell me stories. He told those same stories to the kids, too, but without the detail. For me it was: "She was wearing this garish black T-shirt with, I don't know, holes in it or something, very upscale, and these pink cowboy boots, and on a dare she was standing on a table in the college pub, singing, even though she couldn't sing worth a lick, and she actually put her foot up, put it on my forehead, and you know, I was basically her slave . . ." Whereas to them it was: "She was flat-out nuts. She wore these outrageous costumes, and at parties, Jesus, she could really go over the top."

Whenever he told me about her, he always finished up the same way, by saying that, had it not been for me, he didn't know what might have become of him. "You're my center," he'd say, "the warm sun around which I revolve. Around which we *all* revolve. Without you, there'd be no me." I always smiled when he told me such things, and, believing them myself, took them as my due. But now, as he gazed blankly at the ceiling—he'd returned to lying on his back—what had once been merely a whisper, a subtext of a subtext, became glaringly obvious, a shrieking, electronic billboard. Who wants to spend a lifetime in predictable, orderly orbit?

I thought then about asking him what Jessica's Chinese baby had to do with us, or, more precisely, with him, but I didn't know how to put the question in a way that would solicit any other answer than one that would break me clear in two.

He answered my unspoken question anyway, saying: "Don't you ever wonder to yourself what your life might have been if you and I had never met?"

⸺

Donald Frye came back at the end of the summer, this time with a woman of about his own age in tow, whom he introduced as his friend. Her name was Edith, she had an indeterminate accent, and one glance told you that she'd never been pretty. She had thinning yellowish hair, a sharp nose, a chin that met at a soft point, and a vulnerable-looking neck. Her body was square and thick; her legs were mottled with varicose veins; her feet were wide. Her eyes, however, were bright, green around the edges and blue at their centers. She wore sunhats and clogs and big, billowing dresses, and said that she'd never wanted to be married, and wasn't going to start now. No one took to her—not really, anyway—but she and Donald were seen, at least twice a day, walking together, looking toward the sky. He was as handsome as ever, if older, stooping slightly now around the shoulders, and growing his hair longer in front, to mask a bald patch.

One afternoon when I'd managed to cajole Charlie into joining me to pick the blueberries that grew wild and scrubby near the edge of the lake at a place that everyone, for unknown reasons, called "the sliver," we heard the sounds of raised voices, and turned to see Edith striding furiously forward, her chest puffed out, her bare, yellowing, mottled legs scraping against the underbrush. Coming up behind her was Donald, saying: "Come on, sweetest, you know I didn't mean it that way." When she saw Charlie and I stooping, pails in hand, over the blueberry bushes, Edith stopped. A moment later, Donald came up behind her. He was wearing faded red shorts, sandals, and an old button-down shirt, frayed at the collar and cuffs, its sleeves pulled up to just below his elbows. He put his hands on Edith's shoulders. "Blueberry pie or blueberry pancakes?" he said.

"How are you?" Charlie said.

"Both," I said.

"You know Edith, of course," Donald said, still standing just behind her, his hands still resting on her shoulders. "And Edith, you remember Julia—Julia and Charlie? Julia and my girls grew up together, I guess you could say."

"Hello again," Edith said.

"What do you hear from the kids?" he continued, indicating our own children, each of whom had come up to the lake for one last, brief weekend before returning to their real lives, and I was about to say something neutral about their studies—or maybe it was about how much I missed them?—but before either Charlie or I had the chance to say anything, Donald went on: "Hard to believe it, really. Little Julia Berg, all grown up, and married, and with nearly grown-up children of her own. Hot damn. You and Beth used to read comic books under the covers together. And sneak off at night when you thought we were asleep. You didn't know that we knew, but we did. We figured you girls couldn't get into much harm, not up here. And now, look at you, a bona fide adult. How did that happen?"

"I don't know," I said.

"I know," Edith said.

"Edith knows everything," Donald said, and with that, he flashed one of his broadest, whitest smiles, squeezed Edith's shoulders, whispered something into her ear, and turned back in the direction he had come from, Edith following one pace behind.

"What was *that*?" Charlie said when they were out of earshot.

"What do you mean?"

"'Blueberry pie or blueberry pancakes?' 'A bona fide adult?' Was he always so smug?"

"I don't know. I thought he was fine."

"He looks like the cat who swallowed the canary. And what's with his new friend? Now he's into Nazis?"

"That's mean and uncalled for. Also, I think she's Dutch."

"You don't know any more than I do. You're just making that up."

We had only just started collecting the blueberries, such that between us we barely had two fistfuls, but now Charlie started ripping out whole branches, plunking them into his pail, leaves and all. "I don't know, Jules," he said. "And maybe I'm just being a jerk, but the man has always struck me as being such a narcissistic, condescending creep. 'Little Julia, all grown up.' What does he expect? He himself is so old he's nearly dead. Oh, I know: he was such a great husband, he didn't ask to be a widower, he's doing the best he can, he has such wonderful eyes, such energy." With that, he stopped denuding the blueberry bushes, and sat down on a rock.

"What are you really saying, Charlie?" I finally asked. "You're getting old? I am? Or is it that Donald is too old to get away with the kinds of things that you stopped doing in your twenties?"

"Now you're being silly. Did you even hear a word of what I just said? I merely said—"

"That you think he's a narcissistic, condescending creep. So what? No one said you had to like him."

"You like him, though. He's part of your magical, perfect childhood."

"What?"

"You idealize him, in fact."

"Why are we arguing about Donald Frye?"

"I'm not arguing," Charlie said.

"Look on the bright side," I said after a little while, talking mainly because I felt I had to say something, to have proof that the world had retained its customary shape and texture. "He stopped chasing teenagers. Maybe he'll even settle down and marry this woman. At least she seems to give him a run for his money."

"Exactly," Charlie said, as overhead, a cormorant soared into the sky, and inside my body, my bones went cold.

—

Donald and Edith never did marry, though—though for years there was talk of another wedding on the lake, another wedding to follow the weddings of first my daughter and then, finally, her twin brother, and of Stu Levine's second wife's middle-aged Buddhist daughter, and the various American grandchildren of the French wife of Tommy Tompkins, and Donald's own divorced daughter, Beth—the one I'd known best, the one I'd loved most. On the other hand—well, there was no other hand. Donald's Edith stayed on, and gradually people began to like her well enough, or at least to forget that there'd been a time when they hadn't liked her at all, a time when they'd asked, openly, what the handsome and dashing Donald Frye could see in such a plain woman.

One day shortly after the birth of our own first grandchild—a girl—Charlie turned to me and said: "You know, not once did I ever think of having an affair."

"I'm glad."

"Did you?"

"Did I what?"

"Ever think of having an affair?"

"Of course not," I said.

"I mean," he said. "I could have, I guess. Had I wanted to. But it always seemed, I don't know, like such a waste of time."

"I know," I said, though I was only saying words. By now, Donald Frye was stretching into real old age, first with a cane, and now with a walker, usually with a hired helper by his side—an endless stream of kindly women with various accents denoting the islands. Edith herself barely came at all: we heard she wasn't well. Others at the lake were aging too, tiptoeing into what we all hoped would be a gentle, unimaginative death. They were true, all those clichés about life's brevity. Meanwhile, Charlie and I lived quietly, usually at peace, like two ponies in side-by-side stalls.

I looked at my husband of thirty-odd years, at his dark brown eyes, at his characteristic expression of slightly disdainful bewilderment, at his thinning sand-colored hair, and knew that he was just as big a liar as I—with my remorseless optimism, my willed cheerfulness, my love of the ordinary and desperation for safety. Even so, I was glad that, if he *had* had an affair, he never told me about it. I was glad that he was as skilled at deception as I myself was.

"Such a waste," he repeated.

"I know just what you mean," I said again, but I didn't, not really. Not when I thought about all those summers spent on the lake, me and the Frye girls, Karin, Nina, Beth, the four of us sneaking off in the moonlight, via canoe, heading for the sliver, where we'd meet boys—all those boys, and where had they come from, and where had they gone?—and where we'd let our bikinis slide off as easily as if they were wrapping paper. As we lay on our backs in the scrappy, sandy earth, the smell of blueberries filled our nostrils and our bodies became strange and terrifying and beautiful and obscene, and every now and then, one of us would fall irreparably in love.

The Charlotte Situation

"The thing is," Ben tells Sally. "Why can't I go for a nice Jewish girl like you? You know, someone who can *cook*."

Sally, washing spinach at the kitchen sink, says, "I don't know."

"Or like Debbie Fischbein," he says. "Like you or Debbie Fischbein. Mom's been trying to set me up with Debbie Fischbein for as long as I can remember. Only I'm just not attracted to her. She's nice and all, only, you know, she's kind of boring."

He gets up from the little table in the corner and goes over to the refrigerator. He opens it, looks inside, grabs an apple, then returns to his chair. A moment later he's up again; this time he crosses over to where Sally is chopping tomatoes and refills his glass with the white wine that Sally bought earlier that day to celebrate his visit. From over her shoulder, she can feel him; she can *smell* him. Ben's smell, of talcum powder and Wrigley's Doublemint gum.

"Who's Debbie Fischbein?"

"Oh God," Ben says. His long legs, stretched out in front of him, cast shadows on the black-and-white checked linoleum. "You mean I've never told you about Debbie Fischbein? She's this girl I went to high school with. Her mother plays bridge with my mother, and every time I go home, for Thanksgiving or whatever, it's like: Ben dear? The Fischbeins are coming over for drinks. Shall I invite Debbie too? Only of course there's no real need for me to answer, because Mom's already gone ahead and invited Debbie over. And there she sits, as nice as can be, earnest, you know, wearing a big sign that says Wife Material, only for God's sake she's just so boring."

"Boring," Sally says.

"Actually, *really* boring. Not that you're boring. She's the one who's boring. But on the other hand, she's really nice. I'm not sure I've ever met anyone so nice. She's the kind you'd want as your lab partner or something. You know: she'd help you out, even let you cheat a little off her paper. But now she just sits there, oozing this kind of desperation. And it's ridiculous, too, because she's really a very cute girl."

Sally's not even sure that Debbie Fischbein exists, at least not in the form that Ben is conjuring her, but she's so used to Ben's sixty-second character analyses that she knows that sooner or later Ben will come to the real point, which will be something, or someone, completely different. In fact, ever since Ben showed up at her doorstep, three hours ago, she's been waiting for him to spring it on her. After all, he's come all the way from Los Angeles, where he moved after film school. There must be some reason, other than his apparent need to sit in her kitchen and tell stories about some girl who his mother is trying to set him up with. But Sally can't figure it out. On the phone— yesterday—he'd merely said that he had a hankering to inhale bona fide New York air pollution, which differed from the kind they had in LA as much, he said, as *E.T.* differed from *Star Trek: The Wrath of Khan*.

But three hours have already passed since Ben's arrival, and Sally still doesn't know what he's doing here, in her kitchen, gazing at his feet. He's beginning to bug her. He's already spread his stuff—his toiletries, his coat, his socks and shoes and books and newspapers—all over the tiny apartment, so that no single surface is free of clutter; he helped himself to most of a wedge of Brie cheese that Sally had been saving for the date she has tomorrow night with a man she actually likes, for before dinner, when he plans to pick her up at her place; he's made remarks about what he calls Sally's virginal existence; and now here he is, going on and on about some real or imaginary girl whom she knows she'll never meet. She hates it when he compares her to other people; his tone is playful, but the message is clear. She is, she knows, dull. Dull as Debbie Fischbein, only without such a dull name. Dull as those women she sees at her parents' suburban synagogue, talking about where to get the best gefilte fish. A Nice Jewish Girl, just as he said.

There isn't much she can do about it. After all, she can't change her nature. She is what she is. Any stranger can tell. The short, light-brown curls, cut like a boy's, the large brown eyes, set slightly too close together. The lips that make a smile exactly like the smile of her mother and her grandmother. The hands that know, without being instructed, how to make all kinds of food: not only the old-fashioned stuff like kugel and coffee cake and matzo-ball soup, but peasant breads and pastas and chicken ten thousand ways. She's a gifted cook, an inspired cook. And it is this inspiration that catapulted her, finally, into what has become her line of work. Though she'd thought about becoming a professional chef, she'd decided instead to become a nutritionist. Preparing good food makes her feel relaxed, in possession of her own skin. Which is just one reason why she's cooking now, for Ben. A new recipe, which had sprung into her head on her way downtown on the Lexington line: boneless chicken breasts stuffed with spinach, wrapped in phyllo dough, and baked on a bed of chopped tomatoes.

"I just wish," Ben says, "that I was more attracted to old-fashioned girls."

As Ben holds forth on this point, Sally pounds the chicken breasts flat, dips the spinach in a mixture of egg-and-bread crumbs, then rolls the whole thing up in layers of phyllo. Ben's long legs seem to grow even longer as the light fades from the sky, and his feet, in sneakers, suddenly seem slightly too big, somewhat out of control, the mark of a boy who grew too fast. In high school, Sally was offended by male feet—not just those of the boys her age, but also her father's and brothers'. Big old things that made too much noise on the tile in the bathroom, enormous appendages, ridiculous in their immensity, in Nikes or hiking boots. But Ben is a verified grown-up, and Sally is, too. She's long ago gotten over her distaste for the male anatomy and has even recovered from her two-year obsession with the hilarious fact that everyone walks around with genitals hidden under their clothing. Still, she can't seem to keep her eyes off Ben's big feet. It's as if they contain the secret of his presence here.

Dinner isn't ready until around eight, but Ben still hasn't come to the point. He has, however, taken a shower, and now he sits, clean and newly shaven, in a Malcolm X T-shirt and jeans. She serves him the chicken, the rice, the salad. She pours more wine. The two of them sit together, in the corner of her tiny kitchen, eating: two old chums, bosom buddies.

Finally, when there's no food left, he takes her hands in his, leans in across the table, and tells her why he's flown clear across the country. "Sally," he says. His eyes do not blink, and for a long, frightening moment, Sally thinks that he's about to make some sort of old-fashioned declaration. He clears his throat. "Charlotte's in town," he says.

"Oh," Sally says. "How do you know?"

"I called her office. Her secretary told me. She's here all right. Until Saturday morning. Then she flies back to London, first thing in the a.m. That gives me one full day."

Sally gets up to clear away the dishes. At the kitchen sink, she can feel her blood pounding away in her veins. She can feel her veins swell.

"One full day to do what?" she finally says.

There's a pause. Ben wipes his mouth with his napkin, and then, very carefully, folds it onto the table.

"One full day to convince her to marry me," he says.

"Oh," she says.

Sally hates Charlotte. No: that's too strong a word. Sally doesn't hate anyone, not really, unless you consider the kind of abstract hatred she has for murderers and warmongers, monsters who molest little children or beat their wives. Besides, Sally's only met Charlotte once, and that was nearly three years ago, for approximately two hours over dinner. But Charlotte had had the same effect on her that the big girls at summer camp had had twenty years earlier—she'd made her feel simultaneously belittled and underdeveloped, awkward and excessive. Sally had left the restaurant feeling as though her various parts—her breasts, her stomach, her thighs, even her lips—were too big, too generous in layers of fat and cellulite. She had left feeling that she'd overeaten and talked too much. And mingled in with her strange, unrealistic sense of her size, she'd been unable to shake off the sneaky sense that Ben had set her up: set her up like a pin to be knocked down.

"Well?" he'd said, calling the next day. "Is she great or what?"

No, Sally had thought. She is most definitely not great. She's not even good. She's merely quiet. Quiet and well-mannered and Japanese, dressed in better taste than anyone she'd ever seen. Dressed in real Chanel, with a silk blouse and the kind of soft leather shoes that Sally herself could only dream about: shiny and glistening in store windows on upper Madison Avenue, fragrant with the smell of money. Large pearl earrings on her little pink earlobes, matched by a string of opalescent pearls around her neck. Short, manicured fingernails. Stockings: no runs. Small nose, thin lips, cheekbones, plus the obvious: black eyes as shiny as sea glass, glossy black hair. Utterly and astonishingly self-contained.

Finally she had said: "Her English is perfect."

(It was. Precise, grammatical, graceful, free of the *uhs* and *you knows* of common discourse, her speech seemed overly practiced, as if she'd been rehearsing in front of a mirror.)

Sensing Ben's disappointment, Sally had added something about how pretty she was.

But that had been three years ago, at an expensive French restaurant, in December, when there'd actually been snow, and not the kind that gets mushed up within seconds, turning grainy and gray, but the real, live, 'tis-the-season-to-be-jolly kind, white and fluffy and clean. Ben was in the midst of what they both then referred to as the Charlotte Situation, and Sally privately called Ben delusion. The Charlotte Situation was this: Ben was crazy about her, and may even have kissed her (for once, he was fuzzy on the details), but after a few weeks of ardent wooing on his part, Charlotte had turned him away. At the time they were both in their second year of film school and Ben was, if anything, even more given to extremes of fantasy than he had been in college. He was, Sally thought, able to concoct entire five-act dramas in his head in a matter of seconds, and then, fully swept up in the richness of his imagination, he mistook his own creativity for some sort of objective reality. And even after Charlotte told him that she wasn't interested—the two of them, she said, came from two different worlds, and besides, she was planning on moving to London after graduation —Ben clung on. He interpreted her rejection as some strange, twisted, Japanese-style self-denial. "You see," he had explained to Sally, "she has this very Eastern, very traditional sense of family honor. It would go against everything she's been raised to uphold to go out with me. Because I know Charlotte, and I know she cares. It's as if she's been imprisoned by her background."

Even it if were a cliché, Sally had to hand it to her. Charlotte and Ben *were* from two different worlds. Ben was Ben—lumbering, blushing, Jewish, the second son of a merchant family from the North Shore of Chicago by way of some unpronounceable little town on the Polish-German border—while Charlotte was, at least according to Ben, from the Japanese equivalent of a noble family, educated first in

Paris and then at Yale (barf, barf, barf), with time off for various jaunts around the capitals of Europe. No, Sally couldn't see it. Sally couldn't imagine them so much as going out to the movies together, let alone taking vows of marriage.

Yet she is more disturbed than she would have thought possible by her own agitation. Because when Charlotte finally made good on her promise to move to London, she slowly faded, at least as a subject of Ben's monologues. For the first time in years, Sally felt safe with him. She felt safe to confide her own fears and confusion, and to tell him about her own hopes. But now the Charlotte Situation is back, back and in spades, and it disturbs her more than she can say. Because it should no longer affect her, not really. So Ben's old obsession had reappeared in his overactive little brain. She no longer needs Ben's melodrama to enrich her own, nondramatic life. She doesn't need tales of his love life to compensate for the lack of her own. She doesn't need him as confidant, holder of the secret of her own deprivation. Because now there's Howard Kass, a stockbroker, whom she actually likes, and who, moreover, seems to like her in return. Howard Kass is handsome—far more handsome than anyone she's ever gone out with before—and he's polite, in a kind, old-fashioned way that Sally finds astonishingly touching.

Even so, her sleep is unsettling, troubled by shallow, fitful dreams, and broken by the sounds of Ben's loud snores from the sofa bed in the next room, which isn't really the next room at all, but merely the space— separated by an archway from the front room, where she herself sleeps—that she has designated the "living room." He sleeps under an old cotton quilt, his head turned into her pillow. She feels cramped and swollen. She feels like somebody's once-attractive maiden aunt.

—

Sally's known Ben for a long time: they met freshman year at UMass, during orientation week. Sally didn't like her roommate and Ben hated his, so they made a pact to meet for meals, at least until they'd both made other friends, found their footing amongst the various groups that were already forming and reforming among their classmates. Ben had a dread of eating alone in the cafeteria, emerging, he said, from too many years of being a high school geek. And so he clung to her, so much so that people assumed they'd formed one of those intense, first-semester romances during which very shy boys and girls lose their virginity to one another. At first she resented him: his presence kept others away. But after a while she got used to him, and by the end of the semester, she realized that, in some way that went against her better sense, she relied on him. He was funny. He was emotive. Plus he supplied her with something that was lacking in herself: some sense of playfulness. He didn't take himself seriously, but at the same time he put himself at the very center of the world. He talked too much, and too loudly, and fell in love with someone new every few weeks. In comparison, her own college existence seemed astonishingly calm and free of nonsense: in his eyes, she was wisdom itself. He didn't seem to notice that she was a girl.

Which was also the problem. Ben understood instinctively what was missing in Sally and attached himself to it. Her even-keeled-ness. Her intense, nonthreatening *goodness*. It formed the basis of their connection. While just about everyone Sally knew was either beginning to sleep with or breaking up with someone, Sally herself remained quiet, virginal, studious. Boys didn't even approach her, or if they did, it was in this buddy-buddy, will-you-be-in-my-study-group kind of way. It wasn't that she herself lacked interest, either. She just didn't understand what all the fuss was about. On the whole her classmates struck her as being slightly dim-witted: dogs in heat. Yet she couldn't dismiss them. They seemed to know—in a way that completely eluded her—what they were *supposed* to be doing. They seemed possessed of instinct, and an instinctual grasp of their own animal natures, while she did not.

But that was then. Since graduating from college, and moving to New York, she had allowed herself to go along with what, she supposed, was the agenda: she had cut her hair and learned to use lipstick, and in her cute new haircut and stylish new clothes she had allowed herself to be pawed in the back of taxicabs and felt up in elevators. She'd even had what her sisters had assured her was a real "relationship." But she remained outside it: she was a spectator, observing her own reactions while she watched her date (whoever he was) try to work her over. It was puzzling.

She wishes that Charlotte would die. Charlotte Takahari, or Takirari, she couldn't remember which. Charlotte the Japanese goddess—slender, self-contained, rich, cultured. Ben has told her that he's tracked her down to the Regency, but that he isn't planning on calling her until first thing in the morning.

"I want to surprise her," he said.

—

Even before it begins, the day is shot. She feels hungover with fatigue, plagued by the ghosts of the dreams that she'd fought with all night. Plus it's hot out: hot and far too humid for September. Her clothes cling to her, making her self-conscious. Her shoes hurt. The kids on the corner seem threatening and superior, as if they know that her skirt keeps riding up. And she's angry at Ben, in advance, for what she knows will be the mess in her apartment when she arrives home, after work. She knows that her date tonight, with Howard Kass, will somehow get screwed up. He'll have met someone else—some other Wall Street brain truster with an MBA and an apartment in a doorman building—and he'll say, "I'm sorry, Sally, but something came up." And that'll be the end of that. She wants out: of her job, out of her apartment, out of New York. Maine, Montana—that's where she'll go. Her own little cottage, with geraniums out front. Her own vegetable garden: basil, beefsteak tomatoes. A golden retriever named Petunia.

—

Ben calls her at work at ten, again at noon, then two or three times after lunch with updates on the Charlotte Situation. On the phone he is hyper, almost squeaky. His voice comes out in a wheeze; she can hear him panting, smell the sweat pouring down his rib cage. And behind that, there are other smells and other sounds: the sound of cars honking their horns, and people hurrying, and the last gasp of summer: heat tinged with decay. Even in the city, you could smell it. Nature giving up, curling in on itself, dying.

He wants her to be his best man.

"It's like," he says sometime after three, "it's like this is inevitable. This, and only this, is what she's been waiting for, all these years. Because a girl like Charlotte isn't going to be content with your usual progression from liking you to sleeping with you to maybe thinking she's in love with you to months of talking about whether or not to make a commitment, blah, blah and all the rest of it. She was bred for better things. For finer things."

"Uh-huh."

"You understand, don't you, Sal? I mean, of all people, this has got to be something you understand. Because I know I've been a total jerk, in the past. It was like: when I first met her, she must have thought I was a clown. A big, American schnorrer, trying to get in her pants. Not that it didn't mean something to me, something very, very real, but she couldn't have seen it that way. It's the culture thing. Japanese culture is much more formal than ours, much more tradition bound."

"Have you spoken to her yet?"

In the pause that follows, Sally is suddenly overwhelmed with the conviction that Ben has left her apartment in ruins—the sofa bed unmade and un-put-back, the milk from breakfast left out to go sour in the sunshine, wet towels dropped on the floor. Or worse. Perhaps he forgot to lock the door. He's done such things before. Not to her, but to himself. Back in college. His door left wide open, for anyone to walk in. By now the entire criminal population of the eastern reaches of Fourteenth Street has had a go at her things—her pearl earrings, her grandmother's china plates, her quilt, her cookware, all gone. And all because of Ben. Callow, careless, selfish Ben.

His voice on the phone brings her back. "Actually, Sal," he says. "I missed her this morning. She was gone before I even got a chance to call. Jogging? An exercise class? Because if you remember Charlotte is very disciplined about such things. Or maybe she had some sort of breakfast meeting. So I went up to the Regency, hung out. I figured I'd catch her. But she didn't come back, so I called her office in London— she's working for this extremely avant-garde production company, God knows who funds the stuff. Lucky I got through, too, considering the time change. I made out like I was working on some project with her, here in New York, but that I'd lost the schedule. So the secretary or whoever it is tells me that as far as she knew she was at New York University, which makes me think that she's applying for a grant or something. Who knows? So I go to the film school, and just hang out. And lo and behold, after a couple of hours the elevator doors open and out she comes. Cool as a cucumber, wearing this fashion suit, looking very chic, looking like some model, completely out of place among the NYUers, who are all in black, and kind of grubby. 'Ben,' she says when she sees me. 'What are you doing here?' So I tell her that I have to see her, that I've come all the way from Los Angeles to talk to her. That I have something important to tell her. Only she tells me that she can't, because she's supposed to be uptown in twenty."

"I don't believe this," Sally says.

"Yeah," he says, "I know. She's walking out the door, and I'm following her, talking. Finally she says she'll see me, tonight, after dinner.

For a drink. I told her I'd meet her in her hotel and she said okay. So I feel better. Because if there's one thing I know about Charlotte, she always keeps her promises."

"Let me get this straight," Sally says. "You spend the entire day tracking her down, leaving messages for her, etcetera, etcetera. She's here from London, you're here from LA. And finally she agrees to squeeze you in for a drink?"

"The thing is, Sal," he says, "it came to me, what I had to do, in the weirdest way. A totally LA mystical mumbo jumbo way. A few days ago I was driving on the freeway, coming home from work, you know, and this asshole cuts me off, cuts all the way across five lanes to exit at La Brea. And so naturally I think I'm going to die, only I don't *really* think I'm going to die, it's not like there was this cinematic certainty to it or anything, only by the time I realize that the BMW—that's what this joker was driving, one of those little sporty BMWs with the vanity plates—is cruising up the exit and that I'm all in one piece, and my car is, too, it occurs to me that I've just been frittering my time away. With my job, which is fun and everything but it's not like I couldn't give it up, start fresh somewhere else. And with all these wannabes out here. And all the rest of it. Like there's this illusion that I can escape from my past, from Mom and Dad and my whole suburban North Shore upbringing and all the eight zillion lectures I was subjected to as a child about *if I don't raise Jewish kids I'll be letting Hitler win.* I realize in a blink, it's all just part of my shtick. What's real? I say. And then it comes to me: Charlotte. Charlotte is real. But she's waiting for me to be real to her. So far, I haven't been. I've merely been another spoiled suburban kid, you know, playing around. So I think to myself: she wants real, I'll give her real. By the way, how much do diamond rings cost?"

The red light on Sally's work phone is blinking. She works at Mt. Sinai, primarily with cancer patients. She counsels them regarding recipes, combinations of food that will guard their nutritional needs, help keep their weight on. Her days are typically busy.

"I don't know, Ben," she says. She tells him that she's got another call and puts him on hold.

It's not, however, a work call, but rather, Howard Kass, her date for tonight. He's calling to let her know that it's been a crazy day and he might have to work a little late, he can't have a glass of wine with her at her apartment first.

"A little late?" she says.

"I'll call you the minute I'm free."

"Ben?" she says, switching back to the other line.

Around six, when she gets home from work, she sees immediately that she'd been right about the apartment, but wrong about Howard Kass. Howard Kass doesn't cancel; he doesn't so much as drag his feet, but calls, just as he promised he would, the minute he can, telling her the name of the restaurant and that he'll meet her there. The apartment, however, has been trashed. There are eggshells in the sink and on the counter, and hairballs in the bath; the two clean towels that Sally had put out for Ben before she tiptoed out of the apartment on the way to work are bunched up, wet, in the corner of the bathroom. On the sofa where Ben slept, his socks and T-shirts lie, twisted up in the sheets. The blinds are still down, the windows are closed, hermetically locking in the late afternoon heat. The place steams with Ben's own desperation. He is sleeping on her own bed.

"Wake up," she says.

He moans, then turns over, then opens his eyes. "What time is it?"

She tells him.

"Oh God," he says. "I overslept. How could I oversleep? It's only the most important day of my life. I need to take a shower." He sits up, blinking.

"You need to clean up this mess," she says.

Again he blinks. Seeing him disoriented and dopey, as he is now, always disconcerts her. It's as if the engine that keeps him going at breakneck speed the rest of the time has suddenly broken down, leaving him like a child abandoned on the side of the road.

"Mess?" he says.

"The apartment," she says. "I mean it, Ben. Can't you at least pick up your towels? Jesus."

Again he looks at her, quizzically, as if what she has just said constituted a riddle. At last he says: "But Sal."

"But what?"

"Okay," he finally says, and is on his feet. But at that moment the message is clear: she is Debbie Fischbein, only twenty years hence—Debbie Fischbein as nagging mother, Debbie Fischbein as bored housewife, Debbie Fischbein as the embodiment of disappointment.

She puts down her stuff, then straightens the bed. Ben goes into the bathroom and closes the door. While he's in there, she cleans up.

—

There was a time, one time, when Ben's attitude toward her changed. Sort of. It was during the last semester of their senior year of college, and both of them were depressed. Sally was depressed because she hadn't managed to line up a job, and Ben was depressed just because. Because it was spring, and he was horny, and his legs, while somewhat less spastic than they had been freshman year, still seemed only half-formed. They were sitting in Sally's room watching a movie when Ben turned to her and said:

"Maybe we should try it."

"Try it?" Sally said.

He sat up straight. "Really," he said. "I've been giving this matter a lot of thought, and I think it would probably be good for both of us, for our sense of self-esteem."

"Try what?" Sally said.

"It's not like we'd be taking advantage of each other," he said. "It's not like we'd be playing games."

It gradually dawned on her what he was talking about, but she didn't know whether or not to acknowledge the subject. Because if she acknowledged it and she were wrong, he'd laugh at her. And if she were right, then she'd hate him. Finally she said: "You mean sex?"

"What did you think I was talking about?"

She didn't hate him, but she told him to forget about it, anyway. She told him that it would ruin their friendship. He said it wouldn't, but she knew it would. You couldn't—one didn't—sleep with your best friend. Even if your best friend was Ben, and he made you berserk. It wasn't done. But that night, after he had gone back to his room, she thought about it, and realized that she was flattered, excited even. She thought that maybe she'd been wrong.

And for some reason, that's what she's thinking about—that night years ago when Ben suggested that they sleep together—the minute she sits down to dinner with Howard Kass. She hasn't thought about it in years, but now the scene keeps playing and replaying in her mind. Ben had worn his usual uniform of grubby T-shirt and jeans, and his hair, in those days, curled wildly on his head, giving him a slightly crazed look. She had been full of angst over some unknown danger— the big, bad world after college? Final exams? Terrorism in the Middle East? The night, like tonight, had been hot, and filled with the sounds of small insects, and the distant, indistinct sounds of partying: other people having fun. And yet she and Ben had sat, as had been their habit since the beginning of the school year, watching a movie. She had been a virgin then, no doubt the only one left on the entire sprawling campus.

"The problem with you," he had said, later, "is that you're scared of your own life."

The restaurant where Howard Kass has taken her is recently opened, Italian, near Union Square. There are white tablecloths and muted lighting, and Sally is even more aware than usual of the staginess of what she thinks of as tonight's proceedings. They will have wine, and after dinner, if all has gone well, they will walk around, or maybe go on to some other place, or maybe even get in a taxi and head uptown, where Howard Kass lives. Then it will begin: the slow, nervous conversation, the careful placement of their bodies on the sofa. But for once Sally has decided to let it all happen. She will let it happen, because, for once, it feels right. Or if not right, then at least not wrong. And after all, she's ready, and Howard is—she winces at the word, but it's accurate—a mensch. Earnest and sweet, he has the shy man's habit of focusing exclusively on your face, as if someone had told him long ago not to look at any part of a girl below the neck. She met him, last summer, at a barbecue in the country: her mother's cousin Lila. A setup, sort of, only Howard hadn't bothered to call for almost two months. But when he finally did call she found his sincerity endearing, and then, when they got together, she discovered that he was, in fact, good-looking. His eyes were a startlingly clear light blue, his forehead was high and intelligent, and his hands, kept hidden under the table or in his pockets, were long and tapered, almost feminine. But his good looks were the kind that weren't so easily discovered; they hid behind a manner that was both awkward and overly formal— correct behavior circa a previous generation. She wondered how he'd got that way.

It's clear that she isn't the only one who has been looking forward to tonight. It's their fourth date: a potential turning point, the date that will either be their last or the beginning of something else. Screw Ben. (Where is he now, anyway? Examining his skin in the mirror above her bathroom sink? Pacing her kitchen floor? Looking up from a book to see how much time he has left until his meeting, at nine thirty, with Charlotte?) And the food is good, too. Rich, but not overly sauced, very fresh—the way food should be prepared.

"You know, Sally," Howard Kass says sometime between the first and the second glass of wine. "I really like you." His left hand—with its long, white fingers and repressed expressiveness—darts across the top of the table and clasps hers. She looks down, and sees the still life that their hands, together, make. His skin is white—far whiter than her own—and slightly damp, although not uncomfortably so. She knows she should look up at him, smile, do something to acknowledge that his gesture has been understood and accepted, but for some reason, she can't. Because to look up, to look into his face, and become, at that instant, aware that he's focusing with such discipline on her own, would be to invite a whole series of events that she suddenly knows are mistaken. To look up, if even for an instant, would be to invite him to rely on her, to trust her, to know that she'd continue to do what she's been doing all evening. For she's suddenly aware that she's been chattering on like a late-night talk-show host. Oh! And it's so easy for her, and so exhausting, that half the time she isn't even aware that she's doing it. But she's been doing it all night. Tell me about business school. Was it hard? When did you decide to become a broker? Who was the very first girl you had a crush on? And dozens of other questions designed to make him feel that he's fascinating to her, followed by her own entertaining little stories about her job, or her family, or her apartment. She's even gone ahead and talked about Ben. About how Ben showed up early last night, ate like a hog, then announced his impending nuptials. About Ben's obsessive imagination, and his childish ideas of romance, and his spastic, out-of-control legs. About how Ben comes into her life for a day or maybe two, takes her over, and then exits, until the next crisis. About Ben's bizarre ideas about Charlotte. Story after story: because God forbid that he doesn't like her. God forbid he doesn't think she's just the sweetest, most adorable thing.

"What are you thinking?" It is Howard Kass, his voice almost a whisper.

"Well," she finally says. "I was thinking about Ben."

There's another pause—a significant one? And then Howard Kass says: "If you don't mind my saying so, Sally, the guy sounds like a real

jerk. Taking advantage of you, for years, from the sound of it. I'd tell
him to go take a hike."

"A jerk?" she says.

"It doesn't sound like he's very nice to you."

No, he wasn't very nice to her, not really, not when you came right
down to it. When was the last time he had so much as thanked her?
When was the last time that he had bothered to notice that she, independent of him, was growing, that her eyes were pretty, her neck
and hair lovely, her job impressive, her sense of humor entirely her
own?

"I know," she says.

And then, despite herself, their fate feels sealed. Howard squeezes
her hand. A moment later, he lets it go. As if to say *good girl*! he fills her
glass before refilling his own. In a gesture that strikes Sally as verging
on ridiculous, he lifts his glass in salute.

She is so bored that she wants to cry.

—

Ben doesn't come home until just before midnight, and by that time,
Sally is drunk. She is drunk with disappointment, drunk because, in
the taxi going uptown toward his apartment, Howard Kass had lunged
at her face, and kissed her heavily, encircling her with his arms. As the
city slid by, she had become aware of his odor: of expensive cotton,
deodorant soap, and nervousness. It wasn't that he was a clumsy kisser
so much as a demanding one, and what he demanded, Sally sensed, was
her surrender to his way of seeing things. But all at once, as if coming
out of the fumes of his own desire, he, too, seemed overtaken with
boredom. The muscle went out of his embrace, and his lips, a moment
earlier so acrobatic, became flaccid: warm, soft flesh, newborn. He
pulled back, raising his eyebrows.

"You know what?" she said, trying to make a little joke. But the joke
wouldn't come. By then they were barreling up Park Avenue, closing in

on Grand Central. So instead of explaining, she tapped on the plastic sheeting between the front and back seats and asked the driver to stop. He pulled over with a lurch. "Thank you," she said to Howard Kass as she slid out. "I had a lovely time." She hadn't. On the other hand, she was alone in the warm and fragrant evening, her apartment wasn't far, and she wanted to walk. As she ambled down Lexington Avenue, it occurred to her that Howard Kass probably hated her now, but, because he was who he was, he wouldn't know it.

It is totally unlike her to drink alone, and yet that is exactly what she's been doing, ever since she exchanged her date dress for the white cotton nightgown that she thinks makes her look like a child bride from a previous century. She's been drinking wine: first on the sofa, in front of the TV, and then—again uncharacteristically—on the roof. But sitting on the roof and gazing at the twinkling lights of the downtown skyscrapers, she was suddenly so overwhelmed not so much by her own loneliness as by the clichéd setting she had chosen for her own loneliness, that she retreated, again, to her apartment, and some idiotic show about girls who hated each other.

"Hey," she says when Ben comes in. He is slightly disheveled: his hair is messed up, and his glasses are on funny. Otherwise, though, he looks okay.

He sits down next to her. "She told me to forget it," he says.

"Oh," she says. "Sorry."

"It was the same old same old," he says. "Her parents in Japan. Her career. Family honor. I don't know."

"Maybe," Sally says after a while, "she really doesn't want to marry you." He says nothing. "Maybe she doesn't love you. Maybe she never has. Maybe she merely tolerates you. Maybe she doesn't even tolerate you but is too polite to say so. Have you ever thought of that?"

She holds her breath, expecting anger, or if not that, then at least some spirited resistance—denial verging on insanity. Instead he says: "I don't know."

They sit there like that, for a little while, not saying anything, just gazing at the TV, at what's not on the TV, at what's not there. Then he takes her hand in his, lifts it to his lips, and kisses it. He puts it in his lap, and then, sighing, pulls her toward him, into his arms, and from there, up, up—as if she were a baby, or a child bride from another century—and onto her bed. She isn't wearing much of anything, anyway, so it doesn't take much effort to uncover her nakedness, her naked body underneath her white cotton nightgown. As he kisses her—her throat, her ears, her breasts, her belly—she gazes at the ceiling, and knows that after tomorrow, or a day or week or month or two months later, he'll be gone from her life so entirely it will be as if she'd never met him.

Every Blade of Grass Has an Angel That Bends Over It and Whispers, "Grow, Grow"

Hannah's first husband was a dope-smoking hippie whom she'd met during her year of wandering around Israel looking for meaning. Why meaning, and why Israel? The first, because she was young and confused; the second, because she was, at least nominally, Jewish. Israel she didn't love so much: it was too hot in the summer, and everyone argued about everything all the time. Also, despite its fabled beauty, she didn't find it beautiful. She found it dusty, dirty, and littered. The religious inhabitants of Jerusalem looked at her as if she was covered in dog poop, or didn't look at her at all, so much so that it was as if she didn't exist in the flesh and therefore could be walked through, or pushed over, without a second glance. It only happened once, but once was enough for her to remember it the rest of her life, that a middle-aged woman in full holiness—attired in white headscarf, long skirt, ugly black shoes, black stockings—literally pushed her aside to claim Hannah's place on the bus. It was the number 15. She was all dressed up to go to a party in Katamon. She doesn't remember much about that party, only that "Sexual Healing" was playing over and over again on the stereo, and that there were lemons and figs in a bowl on the coffee table. What she did remember well, and would all her life, was the awful woman on the bus and how, after she'd pushed Hannah aside to dive for the seat that Hannah had been about to lower herself into, she stared a bullet hole straight into Hannah's solar plexus. Her awful hands clutched a single plastic shopping bag from the drugstore containing what? Candy bars? Disposable razors? A bottle of vitamin C?

And how that woman had upset her, treating her as if she weren't even there, as if she were less important than nonexistence itself, as if she were—but here Hannah ran out of comparisons and simply let herself hate the stranger who'd made her feel so deeply unseen. But that was exactly the problem to begin with, the reason that Hannah—who at that time was still going by "Helen," the name her parents had given her at birth—had gone to Israel. Because no matter what she did or how hard she strived, she felt invisible, ghostly, flesh without substance, soul without spark. And then, as a Jew … well, it was the early 1970s, when Israel still stood for something other than strife, investment opportunities, and the Iron Dome.

Hummus. That's what they were serving in Katamon. Buckets of it, with people slurping it down like it was eggnog. Why so much hummus? Why not throw in a carrot stick or two? Funny what you remember. That woman on the bus. How dare she?

A month later she met Olam at his kibbutz in the humid region just south of the Kinneret and married him. On the kibbutz, she worked in the nursery school, and he worked in the fields. He appeared at dinner smelling of sweat and lemons and at night left his scent all over her, in her hair and on her belly. It was sweet and then it was sweeter and then it wasn't sweet at all. Olam drank too much and smoked marijuana from morning to night. What did they talk about, the then Helen and her Jewish Brit addict hippie husband? Nothing much, she supposes. The weather. The harvest. Whether they should start a family. How brilliant and blue were his eyes! She heard years later that he'd died in an automobile accident. By then he was back in Britain, where he'd started. A late night. One too many. Headlights blinding him to what lay ahead.

But all that was later, after Helen had come back to America to try again, this time working as the receptionist for a wealthy macher, who, with his twin brother, ran a small investment bank. A boutique bank, that's what they're called now, but she didn't think that's what it was referred to then. You wouldn't have been able to tell the twin brothers apart at all if it were not for the large oblong mole that clung to the inner wristbone on the one, versus the non-mole on the other. Both men were large, with large happy bellies and large pink bald heads; both made chopping motions in the air when they talked and laughed too loudly. Both were married, with lots of kids and grandkids. Where they differed was the location of their homes: the one on the Upper East Side, the other in Great Neck. Both their wives called constantly with urgent domestic messages, and both men played bridge as if their lives depended on it.

Billy was the elder by three minutes, maybe four, or so they joked. The younger was Abe. It was through Abe that she ended up meeting the big rabbi, the big rabbi with all the trimmings—the long black robe, the long black beard—who looked at her with his big black eyes and said: "Your soul is crying out." Or maybe he said: "You are lonely." Or perhaps it was: "You are searching." Whatever it was, it pierced her. The younger twin, Abe, lived in a modern mansion with a lot of white leather-covered furniture and terrible art. He was somehow friends with the big rabbi, who was there with his wife, who later took Hannah (still Helen) aside and invited her to study. "I lead a women's group on Wednesday nights," the rabbi's wife said. Then she wrote down the address and her telephone number for just in case and, squeezing Hannah's two hands in hers, said: "Can't hurt to try it."

It could have been presumptuous, but somehow it wasn't. It felt more like . . . someone's mother reaching out to comfort her because her own mother was too busy with her concert touring to notice her only daughter. Her mother was a pianist of the almost first rank, and she was often gone. When she got home she'd scoop Helen and Helen's brother into her arms, cover them with kisses, tell them how much she missed them, reach into her luggage to find whatever presents she'd brought home for them, always wrapped pristinely in pretty papers and ribbon—a bracelet for Helen, a shiny red truck for Henry—and watch with eyes brimming over with tears as her children tore at the papers and ribbons to see whatever bit of magic their beautiful mother had brought back from the magical land of charm and beauty as a reminder that one day, if they were very lucky and worked very very hard, they too might ascend to all that—all that magic and wonder that their mother and their mother alone possessed. Little wonder that she didn't stay home for long, that over and over again she left them in the care of their fussy, older father and the housekeeper (there were several over the years) to go flying off to Chicago or San Francisco or London—wherever Brahms and Mozart, beauty and passion, lived. Oh well. Home, with her brother and her father, was damp with depression. It lit up again only when her mother returned.

In his own way Father was kind, and what he lacked in vigor he made up for in intellectual fervor. He was a stem-cell scientist, with a passion for reading history. Which should have been enough—and was, for Helen's mother, or at least it had been at the beginning, when Helen's father was buoyant with his quest and Helen's mother was just coming into her own. Not once did her father complain about his— their—lot. All he said was: "I wish your mother didn't feel so compelled to work so much, but there you have it." Then he'd sigh (he was a great sigher) and, as often as not, retreat into his study, a small, warm, well-appointed space at the back of the house, overlooking the garden where in spring a thousand red tulips bloomed and in winter shined with white crystalline perfection.

So it was hardly a nightmare, her childhood, and this she explained, over and over again, to whoever in her new, Jewish world asked. The rabbi's wife, for starters. The rabbi's wife was named Rebecca and true to her invitation, she presided over a weekly meeting of women, most of them openly searching, some of them in pain, others in bewilder-ment. Helen (still Helen then) didn't know which category she herself belonged in, but she found comfort sitting among the other women in Rebecca's cluttered living room. The room itself was modest: two worn sofas covered in worn pale orange basket weave, facing each other over a coffee table strewn with magazines and coffee mugs. Two or three unmatching easy chairs, each of them different sizes and styles, as if waiting for a visit from Goldilocks. Sometimes additional chairs were hauled in from the dining room, too.

For weeks, Helen took the C train all the way out to Rockaway Avenue and then walked the six or seven blocks to the red-brick house where Rebecca and her important rabbi husband lived. Their children were grown, but now and then one of them would show up, usually with a kid or two of his or her own in tow.

—

In those days, Helen lived in a tiny one bedroom in the east nineties which her mother, still beautiful and still touring, called "a death trap" and her father, now retired, said was "cozy." It was neither. It did how-ever possess a kind of outré glamour: pressed tin ceiling, uneven (but original) wooden floorboards, a view of pigeons cooing on the next-door tenement's tar roof. Wandering Jew plants hanging on hooks and trailing their green trellises from window to window. Her silk scarves and jackets in a jumble on the standing coatrack. Her books of poetry (she liked poetry) stacked into pillars on the flat's single, low-slung table. It was warm in winter, filled with light, and she could afford it.

"Worship of self," is what Rebecca called it. "Worship of self" didn't mean you thought you were God. It meant you'd learned that there was no safety outside of self. That the world wasn't reliable, or orderly, or good. That it couldn't accommodate you. Helen didn't think she wor-shipped herself in this way: hadn't she lived in Israel for more than two years? Hadn't she hitchhiked to the Sinai and, in college, backpacked through Europe? Even now, with her miniscule flat in a neighborhood not known for being especially safe and her willingness to take the subway at night—she, a lone and young woman of average height and build—didn't all of that show that, rather than being trapped by fear, she was in possession of a wild and passionate curiosity that in turn allowed her to fling herself into those parts of the world that lay far beyond her smugly safe (if cold) childhood? That long-ago childhood spent in that classic colonial clapboard house—white with black shutters, the old-growth hedge, the red tulips—in that small, safe, and freezing cold city in upstate New York? Hadn't she grown wings after all?

"It's not about wings," Rebecca said. "It's about our utter dependence on the Divine. It's about Divine sparks. You—me—all of us. We *are* divine sparks."

Sure we are, thought Helen, thinking what everyone thinks, including the bit about the millions of divine sparks gassed in the ovens. And then onto her parents, who had watched from a distance, the evil coming to them only through radio broadcasts in well-padded homes in prosperous and un-bombed America. And so her thoughts tumbled and ricocheted around in her head. Still, she liked the gatherings: the comfortable old sofas, the warmth of being included, the inquiry, the readings—Rachel by the well, the Song of the Sea, *Pirkei Avot*. "Baby steps," Rebecca said. "That's all any of us ever do, anyhow. We take baby steps. The Divine waits for us with perfect patience, knowing we are going at exactly the pace we are meant to go."

Followed by the invitation—always the invitation!—to come back.

Tell me where this story is going. But of course Helen didn't know. What she wanted and what she got became such different things that she was incapable of explaining it, even to herself. Because what she wanted was the kind of radiant glamour that her mother possessed, that she lived and exuded: a rarified air of such pure grace that only a handful of humans might possess it. Helen's job as a receptionist at

the bank wasn't what she'd had in mind for herself, but she liked
the twin brothers, who took an avuncular interest in her and teased
her gently about why such a beauty like she was (she wasn't) hadn't
already been snatched up. She didn't tell them that until recently she
had been snatched up, that that was precisely the reason why she was
working as a receptionist in a small investment banking firm in Midtown instead of doing any kind of more fulfilling work in a more fulfilling, not to mention exotic, atmosphere. Kibbutz Bet Or, on the
other hand, was all that, with its view of the Golan, all brown and
flashing gold in the summer sunshine, its endless smell of citrus and
possibility. The Jews! What couldn't they do, now that they had a
land of their own, a slender fingernail of a land hugging the Mediter-
ranean on one side and hemmed in by those who wished to destroy
it on the other? On the kibbutz, every moment was shot through
with the heady thrill of knowing that at any . . . and so forth and so
on, God forbid. Syria lay on the other side, stewing in its juices, bitter
with defeat, metastasizing grievance. In New York, Jews didn't have
any enemies.

She could have stayed on at the kibbutz, too. No one thought less
of her when she and Olam were divorced. No one thought less of him
either. Maybe that was the problem. That Olam stayed on, harvesting
lemons, getting high, dancing in the long shadows of the cedar trees in
the full moon.

———

How Helen met her second husband, the one she'd have children with
and make a life with and buy a house with and go through two hip
replacements and have both good and bad sex with, wasn't through
either of her bosses or Rebecca or Rebecca's big-time rabbi husband
or any of Rebecca's married children or even any of the other women
who met on Wednesday night to discuss the possibility that every single blade of grass was somehow a literal expression of God's will:

Every blade of grass has its angel that bends over it and whispers, "Grow, grow."

She didn't buy it, but she didn't not buy it, either. She simply didn't get it. She wanted to get it, but she didn't, she couldn't. Angels. Life sparks. The great oneness of the One that was, is, and ever will be. The other women, nodding and engaged, eager to learn, to soak it all in, to have it become part of their bones and membranes.

No, it wasn't through any of them—though several of them did indeed try, setting her up with a brother or cousin or friend-from-the-neighborhood, a series of brown-eyed, brown-haired men in search of a wife who would be happy to make a Jewish home for him. It was none of these and all of them because what happened was: she began, very tentatively at first, to go to synagogue. What she hoped to find in synagogue she didn't know. The prayers (in Hebrew, which she understood well enough) left her cold. The up and down, the repetition, the chanting: all of it dry, boring, like sitting in math class on a beautiful spring day with all those beautiful spring things beckoning while inside you were supposed to care about algebraic variables. Sitting upstairs with the other women—because if she was going to do it, she thought, she may as well do it all the way—she was listless and friendless, lonely amidst their lively gossip. The whole thing, another failed experiment. Even her visits to Rebecca, the friends she'd made there.

She met him, this man who would become her husband, through her mother. Her mother was in town for a concert of Brahms at the Brooklyn Conservatory. Afterward, she and her only daughter emerged from the stage door to find a heavyset, middle-aged Jew waiting on the sidewalk. "Please," he said. "May I ask you just one question?"

Helen's mother, delighted as always by the interest of others, told him to ask anything he liked.

"When your fingers touch the keys—in the opening movements, for example, of the three intermezzos—what is happening inside you? In your soul?"

Something about his earnest question made Helen's mother throw her head back and laugh. "Don't ask me," she said. "Ask my daughter. She's the one who's interested in God."

How her mother even knew this much about her, Helen didn't know. She only knew that when the middle-aged Jew turned his eyes on her, she felt something tug at her heart. His black eyes blinked under heavy black eyebrows. She could barely meet them.

"You are your mother's daughter," the man said.

She was, she was no one else's, though what was so funny—her mother was pealing with mirth—was beyond Helen's ability to apprehend. "You are the daughter who believes in the Holy One," the man said, and at that moment, Helen knew that to be true.

—

It was not an easy marriage, or even, at times, a happy one. David had children, lots of them, so many that at first Helen couldn't keep their names straight. His first wife, the mother of his children, had kicked him out. He didn't blame her, he said. He was a terrible husband, not much of a father, he worked too hard and for too many hours and when he came home he was bleak with black rage. Why the black rage? Because, he explained, how could a man not be black with rage when the woman he'd wanted to marry had been denied to him, and the wife by his side was at best a sort of consolation prize? Alas, the wife he'd wanted, and who'd wanted him back, was from a family that had allowed their son to grow up to be homosexual, had even allowed the young man to attend their Shabbos meals and sleep in his childhood bed. David's own family, having survived the war in Europe, had come to America only to abide by stricter and stricter codes of conduct, stricter and stricter standards of purity, so strict they strangled

life but, such it was, and he hadn't been able to convince them otherwise. And so the wife he had—the one he had children with—had
been distasteful to him, even from the start, and though he'd tried to
love her, because after all if she and he had joined under the chuppah,
it followed that she was his intended, he had failed. Black moods and
fits of bile had followed. "I bear her no ill will," he said. "The fault lies
entirely with me."

David was solemn, a man who not only sought out, but needed
to live inside and among others who sought holiness. And so Helen
changed, first her name, and when she became Hannah, she too felt
every pulse as an expression of yearning for connection to the Holy
One Blessed be He. When her mother heaped scorn and criticism on
Hannah and her husband, Hannah prayed. How she prayed. How the
words of the ancient books by turns soothed or stimulated her. Or
neither: sometimes she simply felt numb. All those words, all those
Hebrew letters dancing in black block strokes on the pages of her sid-
dur. Her husband in a black gaberdine. Her kitchen arranged by milk
and meat. Her hands making Shabbos bread. Her body bearing a child
and then two more. And when her husband raged at her, as he sometimes did, criticizing her for the most trivial offenses—she'd forgotten to close the car windows, or a wisp of hair had escaped from her
headscarf—she thought about running away, going back to Israel, to
the kibbutz, the lemon groves, the stars.

Her children grew up, and her husband sickened and then died. After
the funeral, after everyone had cleared out of her house and she was
alone with her children, her mother, now elderly but every bit as beautiful, with bright white hair pulled into a bun, let herself back into the
house, and, taking Hannah's two hands in hers, said: "How I envy you."

It was such a startlingly awful thing to say that Hannah reared back
and, dropping her face into her hands, let out a terrible lowing that
turned into a scream. This was so unlike Hannah that she didn't recognize herself. But her mother, not to be put off, once again took Hannah's

hands in hers and whispered, "I devoted my entire life to music—to the glories of art—and in the end what did it bring? My children left me. My husband barely sees me. My audience has evaporated. My recordings are forgotten. But you—you have pierced the veil!"

"I just buried my husband," Hannah said. "I'm all alone."

"Never!" her mother cried, and then, with a flourish that reminded Hannah of her entire motherless childhood, Hannah's mother pulled Hannah to her, holding her tight, tight.

The Goy

He was sick and tired of Jews, okay? He was no antisemite, either. Hadn't he married a Jew, thereby becoming the progenitor of four children who, against all odds, decided, one after the next, to practice what they all called, without a trace of irony, the faith of their forefathers? All four of them married other Jews and spawned a whole crop of grandchildren—nine and counting—who themselves were Jews, and not just the bagel-and-lox eating kind either, or even the kind who insisted on some kind of intellectual superiority based on something to do with the Torah, as if the stories in Genesis and Exodus rivaled *War and Peace* or anything Shakespeare ever so much as scribbled on a scratch piece of parchment, but the point was—what was the point, anyway? Oh yes. That he, Gordon Jones-Gray, had, at his age, become the patriarch to a family of Jewish, Jewy Jews.

God almighty. If he had to go to one more bar or bat mitzvah, he'd vomit blood.

Which is exactly what he told his wife, Shirl, when she opened the invitation for the twins' upcoming double-header, at Temple Beth Israel, in West Orange, New Jersey.

He loved the twins—he loved all his grandchildren—but he really couldn't stand it anymore.

"I'll go," he said. "But I'll be vomiting blood."

"You will not be vomiting blood," his wife said. "Or anything else, for that matter. Take a couple of Tums. You'll be fine."

It was a long-standing if not funny joke, how it was he, the lapsed Episcopalian policy wonk from South Carolina no less, and not any of his wife's family, who popped antacids like they were candy. *Jewish after-dinner mints.* That was the line.

"It's not my stomach," he said, suddenly aware that though he'd felt fine a second ago, his guts were now twitchy with pre-released acid reflux. "It's my whole being. My sense of aesthetic dignity. My intellect."

"Your intellect."

"I can no more tolerate this ongoing charade, this dress-up game, this parade of pretense, this frontage of faith, than I can the pontificating punditry of politicians," he said.

"Take a nap," his wife said. "Or better yet, a walk. It's a beautiful day. Take Buster out. He looks like he needs to poop."

Hearing his name, Buster thumped his tail. He was a large, gray, standard American poodle who Shirl had taken to taking to bed with her—meaning with them. Buster lay between them, his snout, as often as not, on Gordon's pillow. In the morning, the pillow would be soaked with dog drool and Shirl would promise to change it but didn't.

Of course, he could change his own pillowcase, too. He could change the whole arrangement. Forbid the dog to get on the bed, or even come into the room! Conversely, he could take his pillow, his book, and his bottle of Tums (just in case he needed to pop one in the middle of the night) across the hall to Jenny's old room. Once papered in a pattern of rosebuds, and bright with the light that Jenny refused to curtain off, Shirl had redone the whole room in shades of ochre and yellow, saying the color scheme reminded her of early morning. It reminded him of old-age homes, but never mind. He left the decorating, like most everything else to do with the house, to Shirl, who was, if nothing else, competent: a good cook, a careful wielder of the vacuum cleaner, a tidier of newspapers. And the garden—that was hers, too. It was early spring and the garden was just beginning to bud out. By May it would be in full glorious almost indecently colorful bloom. Shirl, she talked to the flowers. She sang to them. "Flowers are people, too," she said.

"Just look at Buster Brown," she now said. "Look at those big doggie eyes. He's desperate to go out."

"He looks like he always looks." In addition to doing the little dance he did in anticipation of a walk, Buster seemed to be growing a hard-on, that candy-pink lipstick thing that dogs unfolded from inside their furry little aroused members. In a moment, he'd either be humping the air or somebody's leg, his former humping partner, a collie mix named Jefferson, having gone the way of all flesh. He approached Gordon, his mouth expectant with drool, his hips beginning to convulse.

"Fine," Gordon said to the dog, cocking his head to indicate that the two of them—woman and beast—could have it their way. "Let's go."

Grabbing the leash in one hand and a couple of plastic bags in the other, he opened the back door into the garden, where the dog bounded past him, springing joyfully into the freedom of the spring day before stopping to inspect what turned out to be a dead mouse.

That happened sometimes, usually after a heavy rain. They'd find their stiff, rotting, matted-fur-covered bodies bent around a stand of coneflowers, or lying, prone, in the dappled green grass.

He thought it over. He wasn't an unreasonable man. Perfect, no. Not even close. He snored, just for starters. Also, he tended to hold forth. His wife's words, not his. He thought of his discourses, usually delivered at the dinner table and usually only in the company of either family or close friends, as being something more like explications, open-ended and open-for-airing, inviting discussion and debate, the hearty back-and-forth of true intellectual discourse: the exchange, that is, of ideas. But Shirl was no longer interested in ideas. True, back when he'd first met her at a party—she fresh out of Barnard and he working as an underpaid and overworked legislative aid to the Honorable L. Mendel Rivers—she'd possessed a lively, engaging, subtle, and flexible mind. She read. She laughed. She argued—it wasn't personal. Like him, she'd migrated to Washington to breathe the heady air of the Kennedy administration: all those programs, all that hope! They were going to make a difference, and arguments, all that endless debate, were the air they breathed, the torrent of words their reason for being. Things could get so heated you could lose a friend over a remark made at a cocktail party. Buddy Stevens, for example, how the man gassed on about the brilliance of Ayn Rand. Ayn Rand? That pseudo-intellectual ideologue, and worse, crypto-fascist? How could Buddy Stevens, who was a sometimes book critic for the *Washington Star*, not spot it? Ayn Rand's real name was Alisa Zinov'yevna Rosenbaum, and she was born in Russia: another Jew, with a big mouth, go figure. But as Ayn Rand she was nothing but a reactionary, and worse, humorless.

But Buddy Stevens, he was smitten with her. He was drunk. He was in love. It was intolerable. How could a man of Gordon's democratic sensibilities remain friends with a man who declared Ayn Rand to be "the most important political and literary figure of our day, perhaps even of the entire modern century"? Preposterous! And as things had turned out, Buddy wasn't long for Washington anyway, having knocked up a girl in Boston and, agreeing to marry her, married her, again in Boston, where they immediately bought a small brick house in one of the closer-in suburbs and he went to work as an editor at Little Brown, where he eventually rose to become editor in chief, after which he went on to even greater heights in publishing, in New York this time, but never mind. Buddy Stevens was a nincompoop, from start to last, and no wonder he did so well at the trade, having a knack for choosing the most facile, the most commercially viable and up-to-the-moment—that which would, in other words, be sure to appear on various bestseller lists. Garbage like the entire oeuvre of the perfectly wretched Pat Conroy, whom Buddy Stevens had discovered and let loose on a vulnerable and easily duped world.

He just couldn't get over it, either—how, upon hearing that, once upon a time, Gordon had personally known the then young and extremely undiscovered Pat Conroy, people went into spasms of gushing praise for the author's unconscionably purple prose, not to mention his flights of raw and ugly misogyny.

"Yeah, when we were kids, sure I knew Pat," he'd say to whomever it was he was talking to at a cocktail party or dinner gathering or one of his wife's book club meetings. "He was a bed wetter."

It wasn't true, that the young Pat Conroy had been a bed wetter. What he had been was a blond kid who'd ended up going to the Citadel and writing a best-selling novel about it, and, before that, the son of a passing friend of Gordon's mother, whom Gordon had been forced to spend a single afternoon with, in Beaufort, before his mother lost her enthusiasm for Mrs. Conroy and stopped seeing her. His mother could be like that—she'd take people up, and, like abandoned puppies, cover them with her full affection—and then, just as suddenly, lose interest. So no, he didn't really know Pat Conroy at all, and never had. Still, when people heard his accent, and asked him where he was from, and he told them that he grew up in South Carolina, one thing led to another, and although he always felt bad about it afterward, he couldn't help saying it. "His nose was always running, too," he might add. Or: "He stuttered."

At least he didn't lie anymore when the subject of his South Carolinian roots and connection to Pat Conroy came up. He didn't even exaggerate, not much anyway. There was no need. No one was listening, so why bother was part of the changed equation. The other part was that Gordon himself had grown tired of his story. Just not so tired of it that he could stand yet another endlessly long, droning-on-and-on-in-Hebrew festival to the gods of future American Jewish culture, writ large.

Because it was boring as all get-out, for one, and not just because the this-and-that mitzvah ceremonies were largely conducted in Hebrew, but also because they were, by their very definition, religious rituals, and religious rituals were empty gestures, vessels that had run out of steam a century or two ago, becoming little more than keepsakes, tchotkes placed on the altar of nostalgia. Sure, go ahead, what the heck, believe in your God of Abraham, Isaac, and Jacob, or, if you like, in the Higher Intelligence of the Universe, Buddha Wisdom, Jesus-of-Nazareth-as-Promoted-to-God, he didn't care. Just don't make me witness to your childish need to make me witness your cheerleading antics. He'd hated high school football too, including the cheerleaders, bouncing bouncily in their bouncy uniforms, which had basically meant that he'd had no social life at all. Not in Beaufort, South Carolina.

Which was another thing: the way his wife's family looked down on him—even now looked down on him—because, instead of earning his BA at some fancy private college in the Northeast, he'd matriculated at the University of South Carolina, in Columbia, so what, he wasn't from a wealthy family and even if he had been, who gives a rat's ass? Everyone, that's who, except not really, because who really gave a flying fuck really only included:

(1) Everyone in his wife's family, including his own four children and their four spouses and nine children.

(2) Many of his colleagues at Whitt and Whitestone Consultancy Group, where he advised a dwindling roster of clients on various matters of legislative affairs and the ins-and-outs of appropriations that he no longer cared much about and in fact found unappetizing.

(3) Himself, because, let's face it, once he'd gone from Columbia, South Carolina—where he'd continued to loathe football and not have much of a social life—to the District of Columbia, he'd come to see that the greener the Ivy, the greener the greenbacks, the grass, and the light, not to mention the thumb and the valley.

He and Shirl lived in the Spring Valley section of the city, which was absurd on so many levels that even now he found himself chuckling about it on occasion. For one thing, just a year or so before he and Shirl bought the red-brick, five-bay, center-hall colonial they still lived in, the entire neighborhood had been off-limits to Jewish buyers, which is to say that it was subject to a so-called "restrictive covenant," which restricted such people as, for example, Jews, from living there. And who was it who'd pitched a fit, saying that he didn't want to dwell among such small-minded bigots and/or put money in the pockets of those who did their bidding? Because back then, before the this-and-the-that and the so-forths and so-ons, he'd been, if not a champion of the Jews, then at least proud to have been included in their midst. How perfectly stunning it seemed to him to have found a woman with not only Shirl's undoubted intellectual capacities, but a willingness to engage in intellectual battle, to suss out the grand roiling issues of the day: Communism, feminism, postmodernism, Cuba and Russia and Yugoslavia, LBJ, Vietnam, civil rights, the work of Woody Allen and Allen Ginsberg, e. e. cummings, Nikki Giovanni; how he'd relished the sound of her voice, the sound of their voices, warmed by red wine mingling together until late at night. That she was Jewish was an additional point of pride, if not with her then with him, for the simple reason that, unlike the placid, pretty, made-up girls that he'd dated in South Carolina, Shirl was *fierce*. Fierce in her use of language, both secular and profane, fierce in her convictions, fierce in her sense of who she was. She wore black slacks and black turtlenecks, her black hair cut short like a boy's, her small, taut body ready to pounce at the slightest hint of wrong thinking, wrongheadedness, or just plain stupidity.

The other reason living in Spring Valley was preposterous was that they couldn't afford it. Not on his consultancy salary, which was good, but not *that* good. He didn't much care for the look of the place either, with its manicured hedges and flagstone walkways, its miles of pachysandra, its assumption of well-ordered comfort, superiority based on old money taste. In its handsome, unselfconscious smugness, it reminded him of everything he didn't like about Beaufort, because even though Spring Valley neither looked nor felt like Beaufort— with its watery recesses and Spanish moss and slow pace and antebellum aesthetic, the buzz of mosquitoes in the iron plants, the rustle of skirt against slip—it possessed, in toto, the Washington equivalent of the world outlook possessed by the Beaufort country club set.

He hadn't understood why they simply couldn't continue renting the house in Cabin John, which, though growing cramped with each additional child, had a simplicity about it that appealed to him. The drive to work wasn't bad, either. He certainly didn't mind it. And their neighbors, like them, were mainly younger couples embarking on various Washington-centric careers: government lawyers, scientists working at NIH, journalists.

But Shirl insisted. She was going crazy, stuck in that little house, tripping over bassinets and playpens. She wanted space. She wanted sidewalks. And most of all, she wanted to plant her outspoken, New York-accented, Jewish butt smack down in the middle of where she wasn't wanted.

"Fuck 'em," she said.

He'd loved that about her, too, how fearless she was about matters of class, money, taste, manners. *Ladies of Hadassah, stand up!* But as it had turned out, the ladies of Spring Valley had welcomed her with open arms, inviting her over to their homes for coffee and cookies and, in time, coming to her with their most private, pressing matters, hunkering down in the den, crying, as she listened, nodding, sage, open, inquisitive, and most of all, *Jewish*. A Jewish Jew who'd studied psychology and who, unlike members of their own tribe, consulted psychotherapists, underwent analysis, read Freud and Jung, Bettelheim, Adler.

She came from a wealthy family. Her father helped them put down the down payment, and, afterward, made sure that her share of the family wealth was invested well, invested in such a way that they'd never have to worry about finding the money to educate their children, go on vacation, or buy a new car.

Wealth, brains, and that outspoken Jewish way of being in the world—in his marriage to Shirl, he'd gotten the whole trifecta, including that brash freedom to discard the entire ancient faith with its endless trail of ritual and law, the obsession with separation (milk from meat, cotton from wool, men from women, ox from cattle, day from night, the Sabbath from the rest of the week, the holy from the profane, as far as he could tell, it was all but infinite), and its heavy-handed ethnic tribalism, all that sensitivity to antisemitism, all that paranoia and vulnerability to slights, no matter how well earned. In Shirl, it just wasn't there. What was there was the shimmering intellect, the way with words, the reading glasses, and the books—she was the only woman he'd ever known who read with the same fervor, the same appetite and passion, as he did.

Books . . .

He'd written a couple himself. A couple? Three. Why (as Shirl would say) couldn't he "own" his work? Because, okay, the first book, on the layers of self-importance, rank, and access among the congressional press corps, was a collaboration. The second was his and his alone— a novel tracing the fictional rise and fall of a senator from an unnamed rural state in the South—was disappointingly published with a university press and sold poorly. The third was a memoir about growing up in Beaufort and didn't garner a single review.

Buster stopped, sniffed, and squatted. Gordon pulled a plastic bag from his pants pocket, bent to scoop up the mess, and, straightening, tied a knot in the open end of the plastic bag.

His work here was done.

"Fuck 'em," he said, out loud, as he turned to lead Buster back home.

—

"But you love Delia and Bella," was how Shirl greeted him upon his return.

"Your point being?"

"So why would you want to ruin their day by making a fuss?"

"I'm not going to ruin anyone's day. I just don't want to be there. How can I ruin anything if I'm not even there?"

"Oh please," Shirl said. "Talk about a fatuous argument."

"I believe the word you meant was tautological."

"You have to be kidding me," she said. "Pulling that crap—on *me*?"

"No really," he said. "I really think that's what you meant."

"What I meant is that this isn't about you, your comfort or discomfort level, or your being bored, or your profound certainty that there is no God and therefore the expression of religion is a fraud. It's about a couple of thirteen-year-old girls who happen to be your daughter's children and who happen to love you because you are their grandfather and also because, obviously, they don't yet have the developmental capacity to recognize your bullshit."

Well, yes—she was right, anyone could see it. Not to mention that Shirl was as sharp as they came, absolutely unimpressed by pretentions, academic or otherwise, unless they came from one of her own cousins or siblings, whose pretentions, sense of superiority, and condescension she couldn't see at all, having long since enfolded herself in the family ethos, which basically consisted of: if you're a graduate of an Ivy League school, or its near equivalent (Stanford, Williams, Amherst, Smith, Vassar, Tufts), you qualify. If not, you're second-rate. The same held true going forward, so even though Shirl's first cousin Eric Scholler was an adjunct, a lecturer (in his case, of politics) and not a full professor or even a tenure-track professor, he taught at Yale, and therefore rated higher, on the family score card, than Gordon did. Gordon, who had actually *covered* politics, first for *Newsday* and then, for a few glory days before its demise, at the *Washington Star* before becoming a sought-after political consultant, with three books to his name.

Shirl wasn't done. "This isn't about how baffled and uncomfortable you are by our children's having brought up their children to be Jews, because, obviously, the way we raised our kids left them feeling—"

He knew his lines. "Like they needed something more."

"Like they needed something much more, because, even though, and I'm not blaming either one of us, but even though we did the best we could, and gave them a lot, in hindsight, it's clear that they felt spiritually deprived, that they wanted something else."

"Something to grab hold of," he finished for her. "Something they could sink their teeth into. Something to grapple with and struggle with and yes, even wrestle with. Because, after all, Israel means 'he who wrestled with God and prevailed.'"

See there? He'd done his homework, except he hadn't. He'd merely been around this particular block a few dozen times before. The last bit, though—the Israel bit—was a new trick. He'd picked it up from the last bar mitzvah, for his eldest son's youngest son, Saul. The Torah portion had been Genesis 32, only of course Jews called it by the Hebrew name, which he could never remember no matter how often he tried to push it into his brain. The young Saul, in his first suit, with a clip-on bowtie, had expounded on the themes of intra-family hostility, divine permutations, Jacob's name change to Israel, the meaning of that name, and the ancient, seemingly unending anguish of the Jewish people, which persists to this day, not so much in America but in other parts of the world, though Jews are not the only people to have suffered the miseries of disenfranchisement, double standards, and race hatred, take, for example, Black people, who have had to start a movement called Black Lives Matter, which I, for one, am wholly in favor of, having once been bullied when I was little, I know what it feels like, to be afraid to step out in public—or in my case, onto the playground during recess—because someone might call me a name or even hit me. Which is why for my bar mitzvah project I'm asking friends and family to help me support the Innocence Project, a wonderful organization that helps free innocent people, some of them Black, from prisons, where they're serving time for . . .

By this time in the proceedings, Gordon had had to literally pinch himself to keep from falling asleep. Meanwhile, all around him, people were smiling, nodding their heads, shedding tears. Such a boy, that Saul was! His father—Gordon and Shirl's son—was a civil rights lawyer.

And maybe they *had* made a mistake, raising the kids the way they had, without any discernable religion other than the occasional foray into a church or synagogue for a wedding or a funeral—only come to think of it, the kids hadn't gone to many of them—teaching them, instead, to honor people of all backgrounds and belief systems, to cultivate kindness, and to always vote Democrat. And what, after all, was wrong with all that? It had worked just fine for Gordon. For Shirl, too.

No, Gordon didn't feel that he had a big empty hole inside of him that needed to be filled with anything more profound than the occasional single malt, and when that didn't quell the disquiet in him, so what? Was not he—and every other living creature—a complex web of neuro-transmitting signals and lumps of interconnected, live viscera that somehow added up to the experience of perceived selfhood, of consciousness itself? The human condition is what they used to call it. Now the human condition had to be filled up with God, and if not God per se, then with the endless details and overlapping, contrary, soupy and opaque opinionating of Judaic millennia. All of it written in language so dense with its own fecundity that it made no sense at all. Not in any language.

Despite his wife's family's dismissal of his academic and professional acumen he wasn't stupid, either. Nor was he completely ignorant of the vast Jewish literature: the Torah at its base, and the vast outpouring of commentaries, philosophical tracts, political positions, diaries, autobiographies, short stories, criticism, novels—on and on and on it went, this flood of words from this most talky of all peoples.

"This is serious, Gordon."

"What is it you want me to say?"

"It's not what I want you to say," Shirl said. "It's what I want you to not say."

"You're giving me a gag order."

"I'm telling you it's not about you."

"You're telling me not to speak. You're telling me that certain subjects are not to be broached."

"I'm telling you to get over yourself."

"In other words," he said. "You're censoring me."

"Oh, good God." He couldn't tell what her tone meant: Anger? Derision? Both?

"I just don't like being a performing monkey," he said. "'Here comes Grandpa, the goy. Isn't he cute? Isn't it nice how supportive he is? Oh Grandpa, we love you, even though you're not Jewish.'"

"You really mean that?"

He had to think about it for a moment before he realized that he did.

—

On the morning of Bella and Delia's double bat mitzvah, he woke in the hotel room, confused about his whereabouts, thinking that he was back on Morningside Drive, where, during his graduate years, he'd had an apartment with two other students. The room was stuffy the way hotel rooms are, with stiff curtains nodding toward the appearance of being brocaded, and a stale rug. Shirl had already finished her shower, and was standing, wrapped in a towel, applying her makeup.

"Sleep well?" she said.

He had. He'd dreamed half the night that he was speaking Hebrew. Then he hadn't dreamed at all.

The Young People's Party

The summer after I graduated from law school, I moved to Washington to work at the law firm of Freid and Heller, which people called "Fried in Hell." It was a second-rate firm, small, shabby, on Fourteenth Street north of New York Avenue. No one I knew had ever worked there before.

My father, a lawyer, knew a lot of people around town. He knew Freid. He found me the job after I called home, in late April, to tell my mother that my marriage was off, she should cancel the caterers. "What do you *mean* the marriage is off?" she said. "I've already arranged *everything*." My mother lived for weddings. She had already given three, for my three older sisters. "The flowers are going to be absolutely magnificent," she said. There was a long silence. Then she said: "Maybe we'll give you a young people's party instead." I didn't know what she was talking about.

A minute later my father got on the phone. "What are you going to do?" he said. I started sobbing. "Don't worry, Emma," he said, "I'll get something short term for you. Just to tide you over until you figure things out."

So instead of getting married in my parents' backyard (there was going to be a chuppah made of white roses and lace, a string quartet, a striped tent) and taking an extended honeymoon in Italy before returning in late August to live with my new husband in Los Angeles and work at a boutique firm in Century City, I lived at home, in Bethesda, and worked at Fried in Hell as a summer associate on a case involving trademark regulations. The senior associate was Jim Lazarus. There was nothing remarkable about him. He looked and acted just like everyone else. Which is to say that he wore horn-rimmed glasses and conservative suits, and, though just past thirty, was losing his hair. It was black, thinning on top, and peaked slightly in the middle, where he had let it grow longer and combed it, sideways, over the thin spot. He nodded to me in the hallways, and, once, smiled sweetly to me across the firm's cafeteria. I smiled back. He was gunning for partnership. He put in crazy hours.

After work, I would come home and cry. "The best thing for you to do is get back out there and date," my mother told me. "Isn't there anyone nice at the firm? There must be some nice young men there." I thought about Jim Lazarus, about his thinning hair. I told my mother about him. I said, "Well, there's Jim Lazarus, but I don't like him."

In early July, he hosted a party for the summer associates. It wasn't really his party, since the firm was paying for it, but he was nervous about it, anyway. "The pressure's really on," he told me. "Gotta look good for the partners." Then he told me about his neighborhood. "I like to think of it as the Greenwich Village of Washington," he said. "Very mixed. *Very* ethnic." He lived in Adams Morgan. "Lots of gay people," he said.

He had the top two floors of a new building halfway up a hill off Eighteenth Street. The apartment was utterly without distinction. The furniture was covered in the kind of nubby off-white fabric that's designed to come off in little balls between your fingers. In the corners were a few scraggly plants of the sort that adorn hotel lobbies. The one nice thing about it was the view—of the cathedral, and beyond that, the electric-red blaze that was Wisconsin Avenue, and beyond that, a soft, hazy glow of greenish gray: Washington in the summer, hills and houses, automobile emissions, heat, and the dense wet green of well-manicured, well-watered lawns. It was the Washington that I remembered from my childhood—the city of lawyers chatting on summertime patios, the paper lanterns strung across the trees, the hors d'oeuvres wilting on brightly colored platters.

The other summer associates and I drank beer and wine on the roof deck, and talked about what we did on weekends. Now and then a partner or a senior associate would come out, and we'd all stop talking. Dinner was served. We ate pasta salad and fancy sandwiches, and then, around nine, someone put a record on the stereo and people started dancing. I sat down. I don't like to dance. It makes me feel weird. John, my ex-fiancé, was a great dancer, an *enthusiastic* dancer. He danced with energy, with fury, twirling me around like a top, twisting me under his arms, spinning me through space.

Jim Lazarus came up to me and said, "Why aren't you dancing?" When I told him I didn't like to dance, he said, "Nonsense." Then he took my hands and pulled me to my feet, and we did a kind of out-of-sync two-step together, with his hands at my waist, and mine, flopping awkwardly, out of place on his shoulders.

As we danced, he told me about NYU, where he'd been on *Law Review*. I told him I'd gone to BU, where I hadn't been on *Law Review*. He told me not to worry about it. "Some of the smartest people I know didn't make it," he said. When the song was over, I excused myself and sat down.

When I got home, I told my mother about it. I said, "It was just completely a drag." She sat and listened. When I was done, she said, "I think we should have a party, here."

—

So happy was my father when I decided to go to law school, you would have thought that he'd just been presented with his firstborn: with a son—a David, a Jonathan. To my father, there was no greater profession. "You're a natural," he said. "It's in the genes." During my first year, he telephoned me daily to discuss the cases in my case-book. During my second year, when I was going out for *Law Review*, he called to talk about my note topic. He wanted me to write on the subject he himself had written on, in 1959: Can the Negro Be Freed by Law Alone? My topic was municipal liability for police misconduct. He was convinced, when I didn't make it, that I would have if I'd done the Negroes instead.

At the age of sixty-six, he was still putting in long hours—twelve-hour days, weekends, nights—for what he called the "sheer pleasure" of it. His office had an oriental rug and a view of the White House, and the younger lawyers were scared of him. They called him "H. B."— short for "Hard Butt." He was known to be short-tempered, well pre-pared, and impatient. Stories circulated about him: how, in 1977, he had lost a case in Ohio, and thereafter wouldn't speak to the associate who had been assigned to him; how he once threw a paperweight out the window; how he could give you a look so withering that it made you want to go in your pants. Etcetera. I once went out on a date with a guy who told me that my father was the most despised man in his law firm. "No kidding," he said, laying his hand on mine. We were at a French restaurant, and he had just ordered in French. "H. B.? People really hate him." I looked at him—at his bland expression, his over-large glasses, his too shiny hair—and thought about doing something really dramatic. I thought about throwing my glass of water in his face. I thought about slapping him. I thought about saying "Fuck you." I didn't. I blushed, then said, "Really?"

When we were children, my father used to speak about one day starting a firm called "Gollub, Gollub, Gollub, Gollub, and Gollub." But one by one my three older sisters took up something else, and then, in chronological order, fell in love and got married. Each was married in the backyard of my parents' house in June. Each time the house filled with boxes delivered by the UPS man, and people said,

"Have you ever seen such a beautiful bride?" And my father, it seemed to us, tolerated it, but just barely—he stood there in his tux and tolerated it—but only because he had to. The last time was for my sister Hilary, and I was in baby blue, and happy because I would be next. After the ceremony, my father disappeared. When the time came for the photographer to take pictures of the wedding party, my mother sent me inside to get him. I found him in his study, sitting in the armchair across from the bookshelves. He was gazing at the bookshelves, at the titles of the books. He was drinking scotch.

"Emma," he said when he saw me. "Don't do this to me. Don't do this to your old man."

"Mom wants you," I said.

"Don't get married," he said.

On Father's Day my sisters sent chirpy, cheerful cards, cards in the shape of Donald Duck or Snoopy, cards that read, "To the Greatest (Grand)Dad in the Whole Wide World," signed with their children's names. My mother taped them on the refrigerator door and they yellowed in the sun.

At my last sister's wedding, I danced because I was happy, and didn't care if I looked bad. I danced with John. But eventually he got tired of dragging me around the dance floor, whispering "one, two, one, two," into my ear, and went off to find a better partner.

—

That was the thing about John: he was never completely satisfied. He was always searching, always striving. "You shouldn't settle," he'd say. "You should never get completely comfortable in your own skin." I thought he meant that I shouldn't give up on my dreams, no matter what anyone else's opinion might be. But then he broke off the engagement, and everything he had said to me took on a different meaning.

He finally told me that he just couldn't do it. "You just can't do *what*?" I said. We were strolling along the Esplanade not far from where the

Boston Pops played, and I remember thinking how lovely it all was: the Charles shining flat and silvery beneath a soft gray sky, Cambridge spreading out along the other shore, the stately old buildings on the other side of Storrow Drive. It was spring.

"I'm not sure you want me to go through with it," he said.

Then the meaning of his words began to dawn on me, and I felt sick. We kept walking, calmly, hand-in-hand. We came to a park bench, sat down. "What do you *mean*?"

"Emma," he said, very, very softly. "It's not you."

"What's not me?"

"It's not your fault."

Finally, I got mad, and told him that I knew it wasn't my fault, because I hadn't done anything. "What are you talking about?" I said.

"I think," he said, "that maybe I like, you know."

"'You know?'"

"Men," he whispered.

Then his face crumpled and he began to cry. He liked men? I felt sick all over again. John was tall, thin, athletic, philosophical, and passionate in bed. He covered my entire body with kisses. He insisted I was beautiful. He made me feel special, adored, safe. He was also twenty-nine, a fact that I pointed out to him. "Isn't it a little late to be discovering that *maybe* you like men?"

He sat there a little while longer, crying softly, which really made me angry, because I was the one who should have been crying, and instead I was sitting there, calm as ice. Then he told me that he'd been seeing a therapist. "Because, you know, my family is going to be completely devastated," he explained. John's family were open-minded, supportive, accepting. I told him that his concern was misplaced.

He was clerking that year for a judge in Pemberton Square; now he told me that he'd "been seeing" his fellow clerk, Mark (that was the phrase he used, "been seeing"). Mark publicized that he had recently come out of the closet by wearing a small diamond, which he liked to stroke, in his left ear. He was all right, I guess, but I didn't like him, because he was always making jokes that ended with the word "splewy," which was his word for semen.

"So you and Mark are going off into the sunset together?" I finally said.

"We broke up," he said. "But I thought you should know."

Later, he told me that he had wanted to tell me in plenty of time to cancel the wedding plans. "And I wanted to give you enough time to study for finals," he said. He didn't want to screw things up completely for me, he said. "I still love you, Emma," he said. "I always will." But he screwed things up for me anyway.

⁓

Given my father's connections, he should have been able to do better for me than Freid and Heller. Freid and Heller was the kind of firm that he himself wouldn't be caught dead in. "C plus, B minus at best," is how he described it. His own firm, meanwhile, got the best of the yearly law school crop: the *Law Review* editors, the Moot Court finalists, the honors students. When I was a child, these bright young men (back then there were few women lawyers) would appear on our patio, usually on a Saturday night and usually in mid-July, where they would eat deviled eggs and miniature weenies, and drink vodka and tonics. My sisters and I passed the hors d'oeuvres, and, when we got to be a little older, stayed up late to eat with the grown-ups. One summer, when my oldest sister was in college, she slipped off with one of the guests—his name was Buddy—and didn't return until after dinner was served. It was the early seventies: she was wearing a peasant blouse, and a skirt that she had made herself from an old pair of blue jeans. Bud had a beard. When they appeared together, back on the patio, my mother looked at them and said, "Uh-huh." Later my sister told me that she and Bud had been walking around the neighborhood, just walking and walking, and he had told her that after law school he was going to go down South, to work for the NAACP. When I asked her what the NAACP was, she told me I was stupid.

I never wanted to come back to Washington, partly because of those parties, and partly because of guys like Bud, who worshipped their own potential. I also didn't like the weather. I wanted to stay in Boston, where things were grittier. In Washington, everything was muted, civil. In Boston, people had accents, and were rude. I liked that.

But once I was back in my parents' house it was as if no other place had ever existed, or ever could: it was as if their walls, their dinners, the humming of their air-conditioning, and the creaking of their floors were the sole reality the world could ever hold. The rec room in the basement was still filled with unreturned wedding presents, because, as my mother put it, I "had to face up to the stark reality." The desk drawers in my bedroom were still filled with my old diaries. My stuffed animals still sat on the bed and told me things. *Why don't you get off your tuchus and do something?*

About a week after the party at Jim Lazarus's house, my mother came into my room, where I was lying on my bed reading a magazine, and said: "How's the third of August for you?"

"What are you talking about?"

"The third of August," she said, sitting down at the end of my bed. "You plan to be here?"

I didn't know what she meant, because other than the fact that I dressed every morning and went to work at Freid and Heller, I had no plans at all. Or, I had plans, but they were rather vague. Plans like: think about where you want to live. And: do something interesting.

"Daddy and I want to do something nice for you," she said, in the same tone of voice that she had used, ten years earlier, when she told me that she wasn't going to let me go with my friends for a weekend in Virginia Beach. "Plus we'd been planning to have a party of some kind—you know, like the kind we used to have, when you were children. So we're going to go ahead and have the young people's party. We're going to invite all the young people we know."

I sat up. My parents had a wide circle of friends, but young people, as far as I knew, were not among them. But now my mother was telling me about some people named Holly and Brian, and someone else named Joshua Blumenthal, and someone from Baltimore whose father had been my father's freshman-year roommate in college, and a bunch of other people, too. Then she named a whole lot of other people— old friends of my sisters who were still in town, and their spouses, associates at my father's law firm, distant cousins. Then she asked me whom, of my friends, I'd like to invite. I thought and I thought, but I couldn't think of anyone. I hadn't spoken to my law school friends all summer and there was no one at Freid and Heller I liked.

"No one," I said.

"What about Nina?" my mother said.

Nina had been my best friend from first through fifth grades. We used to dress in matching outfits; we were cast together, as twin doves, in the third-grade Christmas/Hanukkah play. I hadn't seen her since 1969.

"Nina?" I said.

"I ran into her mother at Safeway. She says she's going gangbusters. *Very* successful."

"Okay," I said.

"Good," my mother said, and patted my knee.

—

"You know," Jim Lazarus said the next day, "I'd really like to get to know you better."

"What you see is what you get," I said.

He leaned over my desk, so that his tie—dark red and dark blue stripes, too shiny—flopped down. "No," he said, blushing a little. "I mean, *out* of the office."

"Out of the office?"

"I mean," he said, "these things can be awkward."

"What things?"

"Will you have dinner with me sometime?"

"No," I said. Then, when I saw him blush again, this time more deeply, I said, "I'm sorry. I don't exactly mean 'no' in the sense of 'no, never, never even think of it.' I'm just kind of out of it right now. I'm not really dating."

"It wouldn't be a date," he said.

"Sorry," I said. Then I said: "Really I am." He looked so pathetic, with his shiny tie, his glasses. Little beads of sweat had popped out on his forehead, and he brushed them away with the back of his hand.

When he left, a moment later, I thought about the first time John and I had gone out. We'd met in Contracts—we were in the same study group. So we never really had a date. We just kept going out for pizza.

But now it dawned on me—really for the first time—that even then he'd been dropping hints. Once he told me about some Eastern religion class he'd taken in college: he explained how ancient cultures worshipped both the feminine and the masculine within a single person. "What do you think, Emma?" he said another time. "Have you ever thought of yourself as being both male and female?" And he was perhaps overly interested in which earrings I wore with which necklace, the cut of my blouses, the way I did my hair.

I turned back to my work. I was doing some research on recent DC circuit rulings on the transfer of trademark rights. My eyes glazed over. I thought about how people change. My oldest sister, who had once worn peasant blouses and had filled our house with talk about the Rights of the People, had married a stockbroker and become a Republican. My fiancé, who once said he loved me, never really had. I went downstairs and got a candy bar, and then, even though it was only about two in the afternoon, left.

—

As the day of the young people's party approached, my mother got busy. She sat at her desk, going through her various lists of addresses. These were lists she had garnered from years of giving parties—for my father's clients and fellow partners, for my three older sisters' weddings, for our bat mitzvahs. From these lists she culled a new list, which she then wrote onto a fresh piece of paper under the heading "Young People." I guess it had been hard on her, having to cancel all her wedding-giving plans; now she had all this excess mother-of-the-bride energy stored up. It made her fidgety. It was all she could do, in fact, *not* to return my wedding presents for me. She loved bridal registries and tableware departments, and whenever she went shopping she gravitated toward them like a dog to dinner. She couldn't get enough of it, couldn't stop herself from turning over dishes to see their make, envisioning dinner parties lit by new crystal candlesticks, talking about "good sets" and "everyday sets." She knew all the best makers of sterling silver, the difference between French- and American-made porcelains, the subtleties of cocktail glasses.

After the invitations went out she started to think about other things. She called me at work to ask about the flowers. "What do you prefer?" she said. "Baskets or glass bowls?" I told her that it was up to her. When I got home, she announced that she had finally decided on baskets. "So much more festive," she said. A few days later, she said: "Do you think a cold buffet would work—you know, a little poached salmon with dill, that sort of thing—or do you think people are more comfortable being served?" I told her that I didn't think it mattered.

"Everything matters," she said.

Finally she told us that she had finalized her plans. My father and I were sitting at the table, eating, and she was standing behind us, waving a salad spoon back and forth like a baton. She said that she was going to do a hot-and-cold buffet, with a lot of salads and pasta, and fish. But she was not going to do hard liquor. "Just beer, wine, and champagne, for spritzers," she said. "Don't you think that'll be nice?"

I looked at my father, who was looking at the wall. He was probably thinking about work.

"What do you think, dear?" she asked my father.

He blinked. Then he said, "What about scotch?"

"Young people these days don't drink scotch," she said.

———

I hadn't always been like that. I hadn't always been so passive and dependent. I hadn't gone along with things my mother wanted me to do, just because she wanted me to do them. I used to make plans—big plans: go to Europe, learn Hebrew, become an editor on the *Law Review*. My first year of law school, my father and I had sat down and planned my entire career: honor student, *Law Review* (he said any position would do, but personally he thought being an articles editor would be the best match for my skills), a ninth-circuit clerkship (he named two judges in particular whom he admired), followed by a Supreme Court clerkship, and then—who knew? A spot in the solicitor general's office? A special assistantship? Teaching? "The sky's the limit," he said. It wasn't. Not by a long shot. But I was happy: I had just met John, just passed my first set of exams, just gotten a new haircut that made me look a little risqué, and I believed him. That's why I'd been so amazed when he called me in April to tell me about the job he'd found for me at Freid and Heller. "You mean Fried in Hell?" I said.

"Herb Freid is an old friend of mine," he said.

The fact is, I wasn't the talented one. John was. John understood concepts before they were explained to him. I had to work at it, grinding it out until I had reached some semblance of an argument. And the satisfaction I derived had more to do with the idea of myself as an attorney than from the work itself. So in some ways Fried in Hell suited me. The work was viewed as just that—work, with no deep, constitutional connotations, no layers of meaning behind the apparent one. People got rich there, but they didn't get famous. Unlike my father's office, which was crammed with photographs of himself with important people, the offices of the partners at Freid and Heller were decorated with tasteful prints depicting city streets or children playing.

As for what had once been my future with John—the job I'd lined up in Century City, the bungalow that John and I had imagined for ourselves in the Fairfax district: impossible. The day after my marriage was canceled, I called my future employer and told them that I wouldn't be joining them after all, that I wouldn't in fact be moving west. "Gee, that's too bad," the hiring partner said. "Well, have a nice day." The problem was, as the summer wore on, I still didn't have plans. I didn't even know where I might want to live. Boston had too many memories. New York was too intense. Washington was out of the question. Atlanta too hot. Portland too cold. Philadelphia too not New York. Chicago too Midwestern. My mother thought I should take some time off, maybe go visit my older sisters. My father thought I should stay put. "You don't know it yet," he said. "But you're just like your old man."

"I am?"

"Blood and bones," he said.

—

On the afternoon of the young people's party my mother presented me with a new dress. "I saw it at Saks and couldn't resist," she said. It was a pale-blue sleeveless shift, pretty and sexless, like something a bat mitzvah girl would wear. "Thanks," I said. My mother had in fact had one just like it about twenty years earlier; she'd worn it to the summer associates' party that she and Dad gave that July. The light blue had made her skin look like polished wood, and her hair—which was pure black—had been piled and puffed on top of her head.

"It's to wear tonight," she now said.

I looked at it, on its hanger from Saks, and felt a new wave of depression hit me. My wedding dress—my beautiful, beautiful wedding dress—was still hanging in my mother's closet because it couldn't be returned. It was white silk, what the saleswoman had called a "summer silk," and glowed like pearls. John, who was gentle and sweet and brilliant, and whom I loved as I'd never loved anyone, had already moved to Los Angeles, and had taken up long-distance biking. The research I was doing on trademark regulations was boring, and I didn't know where to live.

"Don't worry," my mother said, patting my hand. "Everything will turn out to be just fine."

Around six, the guests started arriving. My old friend Nina, whom I hadn't seen since 1971, showed up with her husband and baby. I didn't recognize her. She was wearing little gold blobs on her ears, and the same kind of matronly dress—a smattering of pastel blooms—that our third-grade teacher, Mrs. Demavoy, had worn on Parents Visiting Day. She told me that she was press secretary to some senator from the Midwest. "I do a lot of traveling," she said. "What are you up to these days?" I told her about my job at Fried in Hell.

By seven, the party was in full swing. People kept coming up to me and introducing themselves. They said things like, "It's awfully nice of your parents to have us over," and then, nodding, waited for me to supply the other side of the conversation. My father stood in khakis and a plaid shirt by the kitchen door and drank scotch. I wanted to go and stand next to him and drink scotch, too, but my mother wouldn't let me. She led me around, introducing me to people I'd already met: to Holly and Brian, to Joshua Blumenthal, to the guy from Baltimore whose father had been my father's freshman-year roommate in college. Then she brought me over to the corner of the patio where some old friends of my sisters were sitting. "This is Emma, the baby," she said. "Can you believe it?" A little while later, I heard a voice behind me, saying, "You *must* be Emma's dad. It was so good of you and Mrs. Gollub to invite me," and I turned around and saw Jim Lazarus from Freid and Heller.

"Mom," I said. "What the fuck?"

I don't think she heard me, though, because she kept on smiling, and introducing me, and asking people how they were.

I felt like I was going to explode. Finally I broke loose, went into the study, poured myself a scotch, and sat down in my father's chair. I looked at the bookshelves, at the titles of the books. After a few minutes, I heard footsteps approaching. I turned to greet my father—to sob on his shoulder and tell him the whole ugly story. But when the footsteps stopped, it was Jim Lazarus in the doorway. His thinning hair was combed neatly over the bald spot.

"Your mother was right. She said you'd be here," he said.

"Did she?"

"She's really very nice," he said. "Your mother, I mean."

"I hate this," I said.

He came over and sat down in the chair opposite mine. "She said I should come get you. She said I should bring you back outside, to the party."

I didn't say anything. He sighed and said, "So this is where you grew up?" It was really all too much for me—the party, the baby-blue shift dress, the Chinese lanterns strung across the patio as they had been twenty years ago when my sisters and I got to stay up late and help my mother pass the cheese platter. I began to cry. Jim Lazarus pulled a handkerchief out of his pocket and gave it to me, which made me cry harder. When I was done he asked me why I was so sad. I told him about John, and Mark's splewy jokes; I told him about how I'd had to cancel my marriage, and about how I'd spent the last several months in a state of something approaching vegetable life. Then he came over and put his arms around me, and I cried on his shirt. He smelled nice. Like powder and apples. I squeezed his hand. I said, "Thank you."

—

Around eleven, when my mother came into my room to kiss me good night, she told me that she thought Jim Lazarus wasn't so bad. "I think he's kind of sweet," she said.

"He is," I said.

"I take it you have no interest in him?"

"Correct."

"That's too bad," she said. "Did you at least like the party?"

I looked at her—the black hair now streaked with gray, the pale skin, the stubborn nose. "I think people had a good time," I said.

"Next time I'll have more fresh fruit," she said. "People like that kind of thing." She patted my knee, kissed me on the forehead. "It will get better."

And then she leaned over and turned off the light.

Summer Rental

The terrible house that the Millsteins rented that summer was on a lagoon, sticky with the lagoon's green algae. Made cheaply of plywood and ugly brown brick, with a wobbly screened-in front porch overlooking the lagoon where, in the early evenings, mosquitoes and moths batted their wings against the mesh, it was unloved and unloving. The younger children were soon covered in welts and scratching. As for the two older ones—a boy of seventeen and a girl two years older—when they weren't fighting, they were sulking and bored; either that, or they were elsewhere, usually with no more than a word to their mother to indicate their intentions, often returning separately or after dinner, looking sunburnt and oddly disreputable, with scratches or bruises on the girl, and a weird grin and new acne on the boy.

It was August, the hottest, most languorous month. Even so: they'd expected better. The realtor, referencing the brochure she'd sent, pointed out that the house was only let in August, when its owners made their annual trip abroad. "It's been in the same family for decades," the realtor said. "And frankly, at this time of year . . ." She need say no more. The Millsteins took it.

It was hardly a tragedy, but it *was* a disappointment. In summers past, they'd done better, renting a breezy, open, shingled house overlooking the ocean and surrounded by rose hips and dune grasses. The children rode their rented bicycles to the tip of the island and back, gathering shells and pinecones and whatever else struck them as useful and good. That house came equipped with jauntily striped cotton bedding and heavy off-white dishes, and most of all, smelled of something even better than summer and salt-breeze: it smelled of class. A collection of sea glass in jars on the windowsill above the kitchen sink. The worn wood of the capacious dining table. The broad brimmed straw hat that hung from a peg in the entryway. And a single framed photograph, of an elderly woman patting a dog. Before that, they'd had a waterfront condo not far from Edgartown.

But this year things had gone awry—a younger child sick with bronchitis and Ed Millstein distracted with work—and they'd simply been too late. Needs must and all that, as Lauren's English mother would say, but Lauren's English mother had never gotten over her dismay when Lauren married a Jew and proceeded to have, one after the next, five little curly haired and Jewish children (Ed had insisted, as a condition of their marriage, that their children be raised as Jews, though Lauren herself was not pressured to convert. She was fine either way. It was all the same to her). In any case, Lauren's mother rarely visited, and when she did, it was for brief spells only, as she preferred her own life in New York, where Lauren had been sent to private schools and taught to expect the best. Ed had not been part of that plan, but one day there he was, the roommate of her brother's best friend, in his final year at Harvard Law School, and so dazzlingly attractive in his ambition and intelligence that she was tempted to seduce him on the spot. She waited for him to notice her. When she missed her period they decided to get married, and when her period came the following month, they decided to get married anyway. It was only a matter of when, not if. She finished her own degree, graduated with honors, and honeymooned in Bermuda.

She was slim and athletic, all sharp lines. Not so now, after five pregnancies, but she had few regrets. Her children, however, worried her—the boy and the girl especially, as they were at the age when things go awry, and everything was so different than when she herself was a girl.

Such a pity, this awful house on the lagoon—and to think how much she'd been looking forward to their month on the island, their usual circle of summer friends, cocktails on the deck, an afternoon's shopping in town, the pleasant round of upscale gossip: a newspaper publisher here, a cabinet secretary there, Wall Street money mixing with old robber baron fortunes mixing with the bookish and the clannish and people who insisted they'd grown up barely middle class.

They should have booked earlier.

Midway through their holiday the son's sweet little girlfriend joined them. Dawn had long straight brown hair tied into a braid that trailed down her back like a flag, a small, heart-shaped face, and broad cheekbones. A Nordic beauty of the purest type, she'd arrived, as planned, courtesy of an aunt, who'd driven her from Boston to Woods Hole, and from there had put her on the ferry, where she was met on the other side by the son in the family car. Meantime, the daughter had retreated to her tiny sliver of a room and wouldn't come out, their middle child, another daughter, reported that she heard mice in the walls, the younger children found a bog to play in and came home covered in mud, and Lauren began to suspect that Ed was having an affair.

He'd always been distracted. That was a given. The way he worked, working as if without it he'd be deprived of air. That ambition of his: her mother had spotted it from the first, though she'd called it something else, something to do with Ed's Jewishness, as if all Jews wanted whatever it was that Ed wanted and were equally determined to get it. And what was it he wanted, anyway, wanting with such a fervor that more often than not he was absent from home even when present? It wasn't wealth, per se: both of them had grown up in comfort. Success, then? There too, Ed had always done well—just for starters, there was Harvard Law School, and after that, every year's new accomplishments, new feathers for his cap, an increase in income. Was it social, then? Was he, as her mother had once disgustingly claimed, little more than a perennial outsider with his nose pressed up to the glass, a village Jew from the Pale of Russia who wanted to be a Berlin big shot? But that wasn't it, either: Ed's ancestors had arrived at the Port of New Orleans just before the outbreak of the Civil War and had quickly established themselves in the cotton trade before their descendants began floating further and further north. He and Lauren had a wide circle of friends, were constantly busy with parties and dinners, played tennis, skied, and with every summer had their month on the island, for cocktails and swimming and bodysurfing on the waves, and what could be more delightful, more fully a picture of fulfilled longings? And now this—girl. This Dawn, a child with a sweet and perfect upturned nose, the delicate arms and legs of a colt, in cutoff jean shorts or a pink bikini.

He doted on her, the son did, following her around like a puppy and, when she was out of sight, gazing for her, in the direction from which she'd left. They held hands, mooned over each other, and took long walks after dinner. Dawn was assigned a bed upstairs with the next-youngest sister, a girl of twelve who seemed to think Dawn a rare and wonderful apparition, something from another world, magical and godlike. With Dawn in the picture, she no longer complained of mice.

The awful house was packed, and the children listless in the still heat of the lagoon. Even so, she did not understand why Ed, usually so focused on whatever it was he was focused on that he barely registered any family upset or dispute, was so short-tempered. Whatever his other faults, he was almost always even-tempered and—if not mild—unexcitable and level-headed, focused on the clear outlines of any situation and refusing to be sucked into his children's dramas.

But he seemed increasingly tense, and one night in bed he was rough with her. So much so that she decided that she may as well go along because it would be easier than to refuse him. The next morning, when the younger girl spilled a cup of orange juice onto the floor, his hands balled up into fists, and though he said nothing, it was clear he was furious. He abruptly got up from the dinner table one night to say that he had to go to town to get a fax. And yes, it *was* important. There was a reason they'd driven up in two cars, and one of them, he pointed out, was that his professional responsibilities didn't entirely stop just because they were on vacation. "It's called reality," he said.

By now they'd been married more than twenty years, had had the usual ups and downs, and watched as one after the next of their friends split up and divorced. She'd sat behind the closed doors of her den while this or that girlfriend had sobbed out her story—the husband who was cheating with a woman he'd met at an office party, the husband who wasn't cheating but was nonetheless in love with the grown daughter of the people who'd recently moved in next door, the husband who'd been caught with his pockets full of receipts from a week in Florida when he was supposed to be in Cincinnati on business. And every time, Lauren had had the same near incomprehension: How? Why? And most of all, how awful it was for her poor, pathetic, abandoned (or nearly so, or soon to be) friends. They were middle-aged and striped with stretch marks; their bottoms pooched out of their bathing suits. Their upper arms had gone soft, their chins less firm. *Normal aging*, and yet their men held it against them. How could they have been so fooled—and so foolish as to marry such inconsistent and selfish men? Surely the signs had been there from the beginning. *What had they been thinking?*

Good God. She had five children. The pack of them, plus Dawn, were stuck in this house on the lagoon. They could of course pack up now and abandon their summer plans, leave the stuffy house and the mosquitoes and the vague odor of unredeemable molds behind and head home. But when she put the idea to Ed, pointing out that the house was terrible and the children miserable, he would have none of it. "I'll take them to the beach tomorrow, and then we'll go to town for ice cream," he said.

What was she supposed to do? The beach, ice cream. It's what they did most days, but usually without him. So she agreed. "That would be nice," she said, putting her hand over his. "We miss you, you know."

A few days later, Ed's mother, who came to stay with them for a few days every summer, arrived. She was a grand old lady, quiet and regal, dressed in pressed button-down shirts and pressed linen slacks, the occasional summer silk scarf tied at her throat. Ed's father had long since died, a pity, but hardly a tragedy, and anyway, as everyone remarked, in widowhood Ellen Millstein had become larger than she'd been in marriage, traveling widely, attending every celebration, writing copious letters to each of her many grandchildren, and in general having fun when, in the past, fun had seemed off-limits. Now she came with her blued, over-white hair (carefully protected from the wind on the ferry by one of those summer silk scarves) and a suitcase packed with sucking-candies and carefully arranged underthings, her slacks and blouses and nightgown, her walking shoes and pastel-colored soft leather loafers, each shoe wrapped in its own sleeve of tissue paper. For each of the children, small presents: for the littlest of the little boys, a packet of finger puppets made from felt. For the next, a water ringtoss. For the second girl, a trio of short novels; for their son, a sweatshirt with the name of his favorite baseball team; and for the daughter, already in college, a slim volume of poetry and a plan to go to Nantucket for the day: just the two of them, for lunch and shopping. There was nothing (nor should there have been) for either of the parents or for Dawn, who would be returning with the family, packed into either Lauren's or Ed's car, at the end of their time there. There'd been much discussion of it: It was an awfully long time, and was there room? As everyone liked having Dawn, they'd make do.

Dawn calmed the son down, delighted the twelve-year-old, and was good with the little boys too. It was only their older daughter who wanted nothing to do with her, treating her politely but otherwise remaining firmly wrapped in her own private thoughts.

But with the arrival of the grandmother, there was a problem concerning sleeping arrangements. The obvious solution was for the oldest daughter to give up her tiny sliver of a bedroom so that the grandmother could have it.

"She can sleep on the pullout downstairs," Ed said.

"But that's not fair," the daughter said. "Why me?"

"Because everyone else has to share," the father calmly pointed out.

The girl turned purple. "But—" she said.

"No buts," the father said. "You're on the pullout."

"I'm the oldest. Why should I be the one who has to sleep downstairs? How is that right?"

"I decide what's right," the father said.

"I'll go on the pullout," Dawn offered.

"Really?" the oldest daughter said. "I don't mind sharing a room with my sister. But are you sure you're okay sleeping in the entryway?"

"I'm totally okay. I promise. I don't mind at all."

The father looked from his daughter to his mother and then to Dawn. "You sure?" he said.

"Also, that way, I can keep the light on and read as late as I want to."

"Okay, ladies, we all know who to thank," the father said.

It was a tight, unpleasant house. When given the choice of bunking with his two little brothers (there was a double-decker and a twin bed in their room) or sleeping on a cot in a bleak bare room carved out of the underside of the house, the son had opted for the latter. With boys it didn't matter so much, but with girls—especially girls like the daughter, who was bookish and quiet and not quite pretty enough to be pretty—niceties mattered.

As for the grandmother, who'd heard all about the complications, she was pleased with the decision. She had a special fondness for the daughter—whose room she was loath to take, knowing that the girl needed and craved and in some essential way required privacy. Their day trip would be a break for her from the noise of her siblings, the discomfort of being almost grown but not quite.

The following night, the second-youngest of the little boys came down with hives, no doubt an allergic reaction to something in the house, and when Lauren returned with him from the doctor's, the place was entirely empty, silent but for the sounds of nature coming in from the damp overgrowth of the lagoon. The older daughter and her grandmother had departed hours earlier for their day trip and wouldn't be back until late afternoon. The son and Dawn had left after breakfast on bicycles. Ed had taken the two remaining children to the beach. Meantime, exhausted from his ordeal, her seven-year-old had passed out on his bunk bed.

In the quietude, Lauren went in search of proof, something to give weight to her suspicions. She emptied her husband's pockets and checked in his dresser drawers. She looked through the trash cans and the medicine cabinet and even inside the rolled-up socks. Nothing. Not a single receipt, or scrap of paper with a telephone number hastily written on it, let alone a lipstick stain of a shade she herself didn't wear. She even called the phone operator, hoping perhaps to uncover illicit long-distance calls, but the operator had no information for her and in any event it was only a matter of time before the phone bill would arrive from the realtor, and Lauren would pick up anything amiss. Or perhaps he was having an affair with the realtor herself, or with one of the other wives of successful men who owned or rented summerhouses on the island. But all this was a dead end. It wouldn't be easy to sneak off with someone else's wife in the closely guarded social swirl of the island. And the realtor was unappealing. More than once, Ed had remarked that she had something sour about her.

Where, then, and how to uncover the signs? Lauren had looked everywhere there was to look. Except perhaps she hadn't. She hadn't checked the cave-like room under the porch where the son slept. When she let herself in, Dawn was sitting by herself on the unmade cot and puking into a bucket.

"Oh dear," Lauren said. "How long have you been ill? And where is your—" She hesitated, then settled for "friend?"

"He's with the others, we met up with them, but then I wasn't feeling well and biked back," the girl said as she raised her damp face from the bucket. "I think I must have eaten something. Anyway. Really. I'm *fine.*"

"Even so," Lauren said. "You shouldn't be down here, by yourself, and a bucket! At least come back into the house and lie down somewhere more comfortable until you feel better."

"I like it better here," she said. "It's cooler down here."

"Even so. You shouldn't be down here alone, with no one to help. It's just not right. Come upstairs where at least there's a bathroom."

The girl once more evaded, and they went back and forth for a little while until at last Dawn concurred, but only to a point. "I'll sit by the water," she said. "If that's okay? I mean—"

"That's fine," Lauren said, panic rising in her with the thought that—but no. It couldn't be. It was just too hideous. No matter what his faults, her husband was not capable of depravity. She shook the revolting idea out of her head and went to check on her son, who was still sleeping, his sweet little face dotted with sweat along his hairline and his Floppy or Fluffy or whatever the stuffed animal's name was this week tucked up under his chin.

And Ed's mother, right here, right under their roof to witness it, to pick up whatever it was that she herself wasn't registering.

But when they returned on the ferry from their day in Nantucket, the grandmother was nothing but smiles, and the daughter, for a change, was full of stories. "Grandma is such a bad girl, she walked right up to people's front windows to look inside, and then, at lunch, she had a Bloody Mary and flirted with the waiter."

"At my age I'm entitled."

The daughter said: "You see? She's a bad role model."

Well, *that* was a change for the better. The girl seemed to be more relaxed than she'd been since they'd all arrived at the lagoon at the beginning of the month, their suitcases and tennis rackets and favorite frisbees spilling out of the back of the station wagon as each in turn had dibzed the best bed, the best bedroom, the first to be in the water.

Even so. What was she supposed to do about her *husband*? He was a man with a wife and five children, a large circle of friends, respect, status, a house on acreage—why would he stray? What more could he want? Did she not give him enough sex? Perhaps that was the problem. It wasn't that she'd gone off it, either, so much as other things had captured her attention. And at the end of the day, after she'd gotten supper on the table for the small children and then a second supper for Ed, who typically didn't come home until after eight (such were his work hours, his ambition)—well, she may as well admit it. Sometimes she had no desire. And then there were times when she *did* feel desire, but Ed didn't. That was frustrating. Recently not one but two of her women friends admitted that at times like that they resorted to using a vibrator. Lauren didn't judge them, but for herself, she couldn't even imagine. She didn't know what to think. But she wasn't comfortable talking about it, so she didn't.

What kind of woman would he be attracted to, would he make love to? In the early days, when she lost her virginity to him, he claimed he'd only ever done it once before, and that was with someone he barely knew, a girl he'd met at a party where everyone had had too much to drink. After that, he said, there was only Lauren. He loved her freckles and her upturned nose, her bony knees, her tawny shins. She was so un-Jewish though. It didn't matter, he said. He loved her. They'd have a family. They'd be happy.

But they weren't happy, not entirely. There was the daughter, with her dark moods, the way she holed up in her room, reading, or crying. She did that sometimes: she cried. Lauren would hear her from downstairs. The son, too: how dreadful he could be, how rude. Not so much now, though, not since that sweet little Dawn had come into the picture. Puppy love, or whatever it was. It didn't matter. What family doesn't have its problems, what marriage doesn't show wear and tear? Growing pains, mainly. They came with the territory.

As she went about the terrible rental house putting things in order, she heard the sound of the car approaching in the driveway and, a moment later, doors opening and shutting, voices, and then they were all back, all of them together, and it was time for cocktails for the grown-ups and root beer for the children. Having apparently made a full recovery, Dawn sat by the son on the lumpy wicker loveseat on the porch, the two of them holding hands.

—

Two days later the girl was sick again, but this time it happened in the morning as they were readying for a day at the beach—the seven of them and Dawn, the grandmother having departed on the first ferry. She put her hand to her mouth and bolted out the door where she puked into a line of scrub trees that sprouted along the driveway.

The son ran to her and held her hair back from her face.

"I feel better now," she said when she was done. "I think it was the popcorn."

"Popcorn?"

"We went to the movies last night?"

Of course they had. There'd been a long discussion about it, about how the big kids had to take the other children along with them, how it wasn't fair not to, and how, after the two littlest boys said they didn't want to go anyway, they had to choose a movie that would be appropriate for the twelve-year-old, something that wouldn't give her nightmares or be too sexy.

"So you did," Lauren said. "I'd completely forgotten! Even so. I think you better lie down for a little while. Do you want ginger ale?"

"I'm fine."

"I want to go to the beach!" the bigger of the two little boys said. "Dad promised he'd teach me how to bodysurf."

"Only if the waves aren't too high," Lauren said. "Remember? We've talked about this."

"The higher the wave, the better the surfing!" The father shook his head slowly, as if to convey that his patience was at an end. "Kids! Lauren! Let's get our stuff and go to the beach and get in those waves. One, two, three, let's go!" He clapped his hands together like a camp counselor to underscore his point.

How handsome he was, still, with that grizzled silver hair (premature gray ran in his family line), his wide shoulders and deep-set, sea-blue eyes. The still-taut muscles of his chest and arms. The compact elegance of his figure.

But Lauren continued to have her doubts. "Perhaps we should wait a few minutes?" she said. "Just to make sure that Dawn is feeling up to it."

"Good God, Lauren, enough already. This is absurd. Dawn's fine. Aren't you Dawn?"

"I'm fine."

"Okay then. Let's all of us get going."

"Just a minute," Lauren said. "The ocean will wait for us."

She watched as the color drained from Ed's face and then reappeared as a mottled, livid purple. She'd heard from more than one source that, when crossed at the office, he could be terrifying in his anger, but even so (she'd been told) his displays of fury were cold rather than hot, quiet rather than loud. Now his face was flushed and his voice, when he spoke, trembled.

"We're ready to leave and we're going to. And as for you," he looked at Lauren as if she disgusted him, as if she herself was disgusting. "Can you relax? We're at the beach for God's sake."

She said nothing all day, and continued to say nothing during dinner, but that night, as she was taking out her earrings, she turned to
face her husband, who'd propped himself on the side of the bed, as if
to test the mattress. "What's wrong?"

"What are you talking about?"

"You're on edge. You're tense with the kids, and you yelled at me."

"I'm not on edge. I didn't yell at you."

"You scolded me in front of the children. You embarrassed me."

"I didn't scold you. But I am under pressure. A lot of pressure."

"You're always under pressure."

"This is different."

"How?"

"It just is."

She pondered that. What on earth could have changed, what amount
of work could he possibly have taken on that he hadn't already?

"Are you having an affair?"

He didn't budge. Not even his eyes. They remained staring forward, not at her and not at the ceiling or the wall but simply gazing,
steady, unblinking, still. At last he spoke. "You've got to be kidding."

"But I'm not."

"You're delusional, Lauren," he said. A moment later, stripping down
to his undershirt and boxers, he got under the covers and snapped off
the light, leaving her to change into her nightclothes in the dark.

So something was wrong, but maybe nothing was wrong, maybe
she was delusional after all. Perhaps she'd merely had it—the whole
wife-and-mother routine—and it was time for her to find something
for herself alone. If not a job then a volunteer job. If not a volunteer
job then a class, or a new exercise regime. She might take up dancing
again. She'd always loved to dance but hadn't been in leotards since
her last year of college.

But in the end it didn't much matter what she did or did not do
because, the very next day, she went out grocery shopping and when

she got back things seemed to have returned to normal. Ed was cheerful if not effusive. The little boys wrestled with each other in the living room and fought over who had thrown the new water ringtoss the farthest. The daughter, in her bedroom, read. The son and Dawn were on a walk.

The next day she took the younger girl and the two little boys for a whale watching cruise and even though they only saw one whale they had fun sitting on the top deck of the boat eating ice cream cones and making whale sounds. They all grew dark and wind-burned and relaxed in the sun and it was nice to be on the water, all that endless blue water and blue sky and hours of not having to think about things.

"I wonder what Dawn and dumbhead have been up to all day," one of the little boys said.

"K-I-S-S-I-N-G," the other said.

But when they returned to the house, both the boy and Dawn were gone. The father explained that the boy was out on a jog and would be home by and by. As for Dawn, the older girl had just left to drive her to the ferry. She was to be picked up on the other side by her aunt. The daughter would be back soon enough.

"But I don't understand," Lauren said.

"There was a change of plan," Ed said. "That's all I can tell you."

"Oh dear, I hope everything's all right."

"Why wouldn't everything be all right? Good God, Lauren, how you fret."

"What did I say?"

"Leave it."

"Fine," she said. "It's just that I wouldn't mind knowing what's going on in my own household."

Later, she found the son sitting alone by the lagoon, crying, but she didn't dare approach him. He and Dawn must have had a fight. Come to think of it, only the day before there had been a strange silence between them, and Dawn's face was slightly pale. Oh well. Young love. Let him cry in private, she thought. Let him cry his sweet young heart out.

But it was all a terrible raging lie, all of it, and they'd kept it from her, kept it to themselves, the two older children and her husband, keeping her away from the truth of the thing, the ugly unmentionable awfulness of how no one told her the simple truth, but instead let the older daughter arrange and then pay for Dawn's abortion while Ed, busy with work, with his terrible ambition and drive, simply let her. When at last Lauren could no longer take what had long since become their pattern—he controlling, she eager to please—and asked him about that summer, about the girl who came to stay with them, how she kept throwing up and, when she went to him with her worries he'd dismissed her concerns, he dismissed her concerns again, saying merely that the girl had been pregnant. "So you see? She wasn't sick. And anyway, we took care of it."

"We?"

"It was taken care of."

Lauren's throat went dry. "And no one told me?" she finally said, realizing, even as she said it, how blind she had been.

"You were always getting upset that summer. Your worrying was driving everyone nuts. I didn't want you ruining everyone's summer with your crazy worrying."

Nothing about that summer had been easy or right, but it was only now, nearly twenty years later, that it hit her, how terrible it had been, and how it had never really gotten better. She bided her time and thought her thoughts, though, so it wasn't until some weeks later, after she'd gotten the full story from both the son and the daughter, that she did what she never thought herself capable of doing: she left.

The Children

His eldest daughter is in the middle of her second divorce, his youngest daughter is skinny again, once again battling anorexia (a disease that he could never even begin to fathom), and, most of all—worst of all—his beloved Sharon is gone. He doesn't even have a dog to keep him company, the last one having died a year before Sharon did, when she was too sick to take on a puppy. All this, and still his son, Tommy, wants to talk. He wants to talk about the past. Specifically, he wants to talk about what he knows happened, back when he was in high school, when he came home early one day to see something through the big glass windows of the modern house they'd recently moved into. "I saw a woman, I know I did," Tommy is telling his father as the two of them sit in comfortable upholstered chairs, not looking at each other, on opposite sides of the study in Bill's apartment—the Center City apartment with the great views that Sharon had insisted they buy after the last of their children had married, thinking that it would be fun to live in the city again, that they'd take advantage of the theater and the orchestra, and that she, Sharon, would shop daily at specialty shops and learn to cook Italian. But that's not what had happened. Instead, Sharon went to the doctor because she'd been tired and learned that she had lung cancer. Lung cancer! This for a girl who'd quit smoking soon after she'd finished college. "All these years, I thought

I was crazy, because you denied it," Tommy now says. "You denied that anything was weird in the house, that there'd been anyone there. But I know what I saw, and what I saw was a woman. That, and plus, Mom told us."

"Mom told you what?"

"Mom told us about your affair."

Bill lets this little piece of information wash over him, wave after wave of something toxic—acid rain, cyanide, gasoline—that leaves his mouth dry and his spine tingling with some new sensory perception, such that suddenly he can smell himself, and is forced to take in all his old-man's aromas, of powder, and dryness, and skin worn smooth. His throat contracts, making swallowing difficult.

"Why are you telling me this, Tommy?"

"I knew you were going to say that," Tommy says. "I knew that you were going to turn the tables on me, put me on the defensive. That's what you always did, isn't it? Father knows best. But Dad, all those lies, all those years—I'm tired of living like that, pretending that everything that happened back then, in our house, when we were kids, didn't happen. Okay? Ever hear that the truth shall set you free?"

"I think so."

"That's all. That's why I told you. For the truth. For absolute, rigorous honesty. For once."

Tommy is forty years old, a good-looking man, with taut, graying, curly hair, large light-brown eyes, and the full lips of an old-fashioned leading man. It is Saturday afternoon, and he's just come from his health club. He'd showered and changed before his visit, and now wears beautiful soft, brown corduroy trousers, a white button-down shirt, and a well-made if somewhat threadbare tweed jacket. Ever since he'd been a child, he's blamed Bill for his problems: struggles in school and on the sports fields, difficulties with relationships, career worries, anxiety. Even so, he seems to have come out all right, with a good job, and a pretty, blond Christian wife who spends most of her time, when she, too, isn't exercising, working for the rights of Sudanese women. No children, though. Apparently neither one of them wants them, which is another thing Bill can't understand about his son. Not want children of your own? He himself had relished the arrival of each of his children, standing over their cribs in a swoon of wonder.

"What is it you want from me, son?"

Tommy gets up and stretches, his arms held overhead like a dancer's, before collapsing back in the chair. There's something soft, almost feminine, about this one son of his, something overly refined, overly fussy, almost feline, as if, despite the hours he puts in at the gym, he'd never worked his muscles hard enough, or broken a sweat.

"That's just it," Tommy says. "I don't want anything from you. Not even an apology. And I certainly don't want you to take me out to dinner or buy me a present." Bill winces, thinking of all the times he and Sharon had done just that, buying things—sports equipment, theater tickets, even furniture—that they thought Tommy would like. They did it occasionally for the girls, too, but that had mainly been Sharon's department: she'd liked nothing better than surprising one or the other of them with an antique quilt that she thought they'd like, or table linens, or a complete set of stemware that matched their wedding China. (Sharon remembered things like that, even after first their first daughter and then their second went through ugly, painful, expensive, drawn-out divorces.) It was as if she believed that, provided with the proper trappings of the right kind of life, all would be well for them. But it wasn't. As they entered their middle years, all three of their children seemed perpetually unmoored, with a neediness, a lack of something that Bill can neither locate nor understand. "It was tough on Mom."

"Your mother told you this?"

Tommy shrugs. Bill can smell the aftershave on him. A lemony smell, like furniture polish. "She told all three of us," Tommy says. "When she got sick, that is. Not right away. It was later, when she began to realize how bad it was."

"Later?" Bill says, thinking of her last weeks, when she lay, zonked out on painkillers and bloated like a rotting pumpkin on the bed in the small back bedroom of their apartment, where a nurse watched over her day and night, and a stream of visitors came to sit with her, holding her hand and talking to her as if she could still hear them.

"When she realized that she was dying," Tommy says.

"I see."

"She was tired of covering for you."

Now it's Bill's turn to get up. What else is there to do? Turning away from his son, he gazes out the window. It's a dark, overcast day, the clouds low, gray on their underbellies and urine-colored above, casting a queasy yellow light over the city, its traffic and streets, its row houses and parks, its trees now in flagrant, raucous bloom. Life struggling to reclaim itself. Sharon had loved this view.

"And that's another thing, Dad," Tommy continues, speaking to his back. "It was like, when we were kids, we were supposed to think that we were the perfect family. Two girls and a boy, not to mention the golden retrievers. Like we were part of a package, an image that you put together, you and Mom both, of the perfect American family. Like the three of us were no more than lifestyle accessories."

"I really don't think that's fair."

"Can you deny it? Okay. I'll ask you a question. What role did I play in *The Mikado*?"

"What?"

"*The Mikado*. A play by Gilbert and Sullivan. My class put it on in the seventh grade. It was a big deal. We got a write-up in the local paper."

Vaguely, it comes back to him now—his son in makeup, with blue eyeshadow covering his eyelids, and bright red lipstick on his cheeks. For months, he'd gone around the house singing. But the exact part? He can barely remember the address of the house he'd grown up in.

"I don't know, Tommy."

"Of course you don't know, Dad, and you want to know why? You don't know because you weren't there."

"That's inaccurate. Mom and I attended all your school plays, and everything else too. Piano recitals. Soccer games. Track meets. We were there for all of it."

"Wrong again, Dad. Mom was there. You were at work. Or wherever."

The Mikado? Was he kidding? But five minutes after Tommy leaves, it comes back to him: Tommy had been the Mikado himself, resplendent in silk on thick cushions.

—

The truth may or may not set you free, but with Sharon gone, he no longer cared about such niceties. He'd been deeply in love with her but as the years had worn on, their marriage had become routine, which in and of itself wasn't so terrible. But when life took on a gray flatness, a crushing burden of mediocrity, he'd begun to feel trapped. And then, because it had presented itself to him, he'd had an affair.

A single, short-lived affair. A few months of thrills before spending the rest of his life back inside his marriage, doing his plodding, dull, steady best to be the husband Sharon wanted him to be. And then, his final act of contrition, when he'd taken early retirement so he could take care of her. He'd loved his job, but that was that. Sharon came first.

She'd spilled the beans to the kids anyway, and never mentioned a thing about it to him. Which was amazing, given how much she'd talked during those last few months—telling him over and over again how she wasn't afraid to die, but rather, was merely sad: sad because she wouldn't be able to attend all those birthdays and bar mitzvahs, graduations and weddings. How much she'd miss everyone, she'd say over and over, as if the dead, moldering in the ground, remembered. She told him that she'd always loved him and believed in him, and also said that as her time drew near she saw, with the clarity of a saint or a psychic, the mistakes that she herself had made out of her own wounded egoism, her own unfinished parts. She talked about boundaries, about unmet needs, confessing that she'd spoiled and overprotected the kids, that she'd worried too much about what other people thought of her. Toward the very end of the very end of her life, she told him that she'd forgiven him long ago for what she still referred to as *that time.* "Because it forced me to grow," she said.

"It's all a passing show anyhow. All over in the blink of an eye! It's all exactly as it was meant to be. I married you because I needed to learn the lessons I learned."

She talked about more practical things too—about how she wanted her jewelry distributed, about how Bill might go about hiring someone who could both cook and clean for him, because God knows, without a steady hand running the household, the apartment would soon fall into utter ruination. She made him promise not to stay home and brood, but rather, go out—take classes at Penn, go to the gym. Anything other than sit around that moldy old synagogue of his, thinking about his father.

And again, she'd be off and running, the words overflowing her mouth—that father of his who was just so mean, so mean and so rigid and so quick to find fault—and was it any wonder that Bill, who never felt like he was good enough, tried to fill the hole in his insides by having an affair? But in all that tumult of talk, she'd never once mentioned that she'd told the children about Clara Stein.

—

Despite his promise, every morning, he dons his tallit and his phylacteries and goes down to the old shul, his father's shul, where he'd gone as a kid. Considering what the intervening years had done to the neighborhood, turning it, first, into a slum, and then into a yuppie paradise of coffee shops and overpriced boutiques, it amazed him that it was still there. And there he prayed, an old man alone among other old men, the young people—his own son included—apparently too busy with their own pursuits to remember their dead.

It is as it always was: small, dark, cramped, smelling of oil and wool and damp socks and, oddly, of smoke. In the old days, the women sat upstairs, in the gallery, but now the gallery is empty, and what few women there are sit with everyone else. It was here that he'd come, with his father and uncle, every Saturday morning for most of his childhood, the sole boy among the cousins, the weight of four thousand years of Jewish history and untold distant European relatives who'd gone up in smoke pressing on his shoulders and squeezing the top of his head. But he, Bill, was a child of America, hopeful, optimistic, with dirty blond hair, hazel eyes, and quick reflexes, a high school track star, a good dancer. Who would have ever thought that a Jewish boy could have grown up so straight and tall, with such graceful, languid arms and legs, and such a wide-open face? Funny, too, because the fact of the matter was that Bill's father, Max, was native-born, as much a child of Philadelphia as Betsy Ross herself. Even so, Max Bacher was a greenhorn. A native-born greenhorn. An American who didn't know what his nationality was. How mean he was, too. Mean to his wife, mean to his daughters, mean to Bill. Nothing, it seemed, was good enough for him. The only time he laughed was when he talked about the Marx Brothers.

Master of the Universe! God and God of my fathers! What do my children want of me?

Yitgadal, v'yitkadash, shmay, rabbaw . . .

—

Her name was Clara Stein. An old-fashioned name, and yet she wasn't old-fashioned in the least. Divorced, and with a good head for business, she played tennis, loved the blues, and swore. She had smooth dark brown hair that she wore in a kind of bob, a long graceful neck, thick arching eyebrows, blood-red fingernails, and a daughter who'd just started college. She owned a bookstore one town over. It was there that he'd met her; he'd just dropped the children off at Sunday school and stopped at the bookstore to pick up a book that Sharon wanted. When he couldn't find it, Clara ordered it for him, taking down his name and telephone number.

The affair started on the day that Bill drove to the bookshop after hours to pick up Sharon's book. It was on his way home from work anyway, and Clara has assured him that though the shop was closed, she needed to stay late to work on inventory. Their connection was instantaneous, and not just sexually. They talked about everything from reincarnation to the failures of socialism to the limits of human intelligence. Bill was no intellectual, but he had managed to scrap together an education for himself, first at Temple, and later—after he'd done so well that he could move his family into the sparkling modern house with its floor-to-ceiling windows—within the confines of his own study. How wonderful to have a study—to be able to lead guests over the polished dark flagstones of the hallway to admire the small room at the back of the house where, on the weekends and after work, he liked to sit and read. There, along one wall, were the built-in bookcases that Sharon had had made, and within them his lovingly curated collection. He especially loved reading history, gobbling up centuries at a time, insatiably curious about the story of humankind.

In the West Philadelphia neighborhood where he'd grown up, people talked about politics, the weather, the Jews, and their health. It was much the same at home, with his father complaining about his bowels, and his mother yelling at him to eat more fresh fruit. His own bowel movements, come to think of it, were also a subject of some concern, his mother inquiring every now and then if he were regular. In the winter months, the conversation turned to throats. Throats and noses: coughs and colds.

Sharon was from the neighborhood, too, only he hadn't known her when they were growing up. He'd met her later, when he was at Temple and she was a scholarship student, studying education, at Drexel. He'd been set up with her roommate on a double blind date. His friend Irving Wachshaw had been Sharon's date. The four of them had gone out for Italian. She had red hair and perfect square teeth and a satin-soft white neck. He'd fallen in love with her almost immediately.

—

After her death, he'd had hundreds of thank you notes to write. Who would have ever guessed that Sharon had inspired so much affection? But apparently she had, because there they were—the sympathy notes from former students, from girls she'd gone to school with, the checks made out to the American Cancer Society and the Save the Parks program in Sharon's honor, notes from the parents of their children's childhood friends, letters from women she'd known from the PTA and the Federation, from her cooking classes and the one semester that she'd gone back to school, thinking that maybe she wanted to get a master's degree in special ed. He even got one from Clara Stein, a brief note, saying that she was sending prayers. He'd answered her, and every other of those notes as well, sending out tasteful cards on thick creamy paper with the words "The Family of Sharon Bacher" on the front and his own personal message on the back, as his Waspy daughter-in-law, Eleanor, had suggested he do. To Clara Stein he'd only written "Thank you."

She lived in the same house she'd lived in when they'd been lovers: it was the return address on her note to him. Apparently she'd never remarried, and never, as far as he knew, embarked on another love affair. Not that they kept in touch. Even before Sharon had confronted him with evidence of his betrayal, he and Clara had been drifting away from each other by the pressures of everyday life. How old would she be now? Seventy-six? Seventy-seven? She must have seen Sharon's obituary, or heard talk of it in her bookstore.

He was tempted to call her, but instead, sat in the synagogue, yearning.

Heavenly Father that You may forgive me! You give me life, and I fritter it away. You give me children, and they grow up as trees bent by the wind; You give me a wife, and I loved her but was bored with marriage—and now she is torn from me, and I have no one to whom I might turn.

She's been gone for more than a year.

—

"He shouldn't have said what he said to you. He shouldn't have said anything." It's his oldest daughter, Natalie, on the phone, shouting to be heard over the sound of her children, who were fighting in the background. Her first husband had left her twelve years ago, saying that he wasn't cut out for marriage. The second tended toward depression and was frequently unemployed, and she threw him out. She liked to give advice anyhow. Thank God she herself had a job: in fact, she did better than that. She owned a clothing boutique that was wildly popular with the private-school-girl set in her town, selling them inexpensive fashionable jewelry and ripped jeans that rested beneath their navels.

"I swear to God, I'm going to have to slap these two boys silly," she said. Then: "I'm talking to Poppa Bill, all right? Who do you think I'm talking to?" Bill waited. "But anyway, back to Tommy. I don't know, Dad. He just should have kept his big mouth shut, okay. I mean, what's done is done. Ancient history, and all that."

He's uncomfortable when Natalie talks to him like this, like she's his mother, or like he's an imbecile. But he doesn't interrupt. Natalie and her brother had never been close, and in recent years, they had all but declared out-and-out war on each other. He could never be exactly sure why they bickered so vehemently, but he suspected that it all boiled down to disagreements about their mother's last months, as if, even as Sharon slid further and further into the land of the dying, it was their duty, as siblings, to win the lion's share of her love.

"He asked me if I remembered what part he'd played in *The Mikado*."

"Jesus Christ. How is anyone supposed to remember that?"

"He played the Mikado, actually," Bill says.

"But it doesn't matter, Dad. The point is—well, you know what the point is. The point is that Mom's gone, and nothing's going to change that, and in the meantime, what happened between the two of you isn't anybody's business but your own."

"I appreciate that," Bill says, though what he really would appreciate would have been that Sharon had kept her peace, or because it was too late for that, silence on the part of his children. Yes, he'd cheated. But all three of them had done worse, sleeping around in college and afterward, experimenting with drugs, the whole generation nine yards of stupidity masquerading as freedom. After all, who was it who had paid for rehab when Tommy had had that little problem with cocaine? And shelled out again when Jill started attempting to starve herself to death? Come to think about it, he'd paid for her divorce lawyer, too. But what could he do? He couldn't simply let them go to pieces. He was their father. It was the father's job to take care of the children.

—

Even now he doesn't know how or why he'd so abruptly turned his back on his wife and children, forsaken his wedding vows, and broken with Jewish law. It was almost as if he'd been under the influence of a drug. During the whole of his affair, he'd been tormented with guilt, suffering first from stomachaches, then from headaches, then from sleeplessness. So guilty had he felt that he was almost relieved when Sharon had found evidence of Clara in the form of a receipt from a downtown restaurant. He'd been telling her, the entire time, that he was going to the gym—working out. An easy lie, particularly since he'd lost weight, as if his desire for Clara had burned a hole not only in his soul, but his gut, too. Whereas his love for Sharon—and he'd loved her, steadily, even at the height of his affair with Clara—was more like a child's love for the onset of spring.

She'd caused a scene, all right, waiving the receipt in his face, her face contorted, her mouth wide open and screaming as if she were in labor. She'd known it, she'd said. She'd known about it all along. "I even started seeing a therapist," she said, her eyes pink from crying. "I thought I was going crazy but all along it wasn't me, it was you!" Even after he'd broken things off with Clara, she'd continued to see him, coming home with bits of wisdom she'd gleaned from her therapy sessions. "Relationships are a dance." "Without trust, it's like walking on eggshells."

They got through it. They got through it by Sharon taking a part-time job that she liked, as a tutor in a private school. They got through it by waiting. They got through it by making dates. They got through it by Sharon talking and Bill listening. He continued listening all through the next decades with their kids growing up and having children of their own, and then, during the final months, as she lay dying. "I know you don't think you'll want to remarry, but face it, Bill, you're not going to be able to stay single for more than ten minutes," she liked to say. He protested, but his protests only made her insist more strenuously. She even drew up a list of eligible widows and divorcees for him. "Just promise me one thing," she said. "Just promise me that you won't marry that stuck up Clara. Talk about pretentious. She never was for you, you knew that, didn't you?"

What could he say? As he sat, day after day, holding Sharon's hand, and watching ancient television reruns with her on cable, the last thing on his mind was Clara Stein. Not that he'd blocked out all thoughts of her. It wasn't possible. On occasion, he even dreamed of her, sometimes with such piercing longing, and such amazing detail, that when he woke he was amazed by the clarity of his subconsciousness, how it conjured, with such miraculous detail, the way Clara had looked, talked, and behaved; the tilt of her head, the smell of her perfume. Even during Sharon's last weeks (and any fool could have seen that, as fall had turned to winter, Sharon had no more than a month or two left) Clara had, on occasion, popped up in his dreams, leaving him, upon waking, with a lasting impression of both pleasure and pain.

—

This time it's Jill who wants to talk. But not on the phone or at the apartment or her place. Nor at a restaurant or coffeehouse, either, but rather, someplace open and outside, neutral, she says, because what she has to say is difficult, and she's not sure she can tell him at too close a range. Which makes Bill wonder how she plans to talk to him at all: perhaps by shouting to him across a field?

He agrees to meet her near the boathouses in Fairmont Park. She is waiting for him at the designated spot, leaning up against a statue of William Penn, her head nodding to music pumped into her ears from her iPod. The wonders of technology, he muses: now none of us ever have to read, converse, or think. But then he stops himself: What a grouch I've become! A replica of my own father! Just then Jill, glancing up, notices him and waves.

Dressed in jeans and a long-sleeved T-shirt, with running shoes on her feet and a faded jean jacket over her shoulders, her long, straw-colored hair pulled back into a ponytail, from a distance Jill looks like a lanky adolescent, a young girl who still hasn't caught up to her growth spurt. She's no girl however, but a woman of thirty-five. She is no longer starving herself, but she's too thin—a child could see that—with breasts no bigger than wafers and cheekbones that cut her face like ritual markings. Why she refuses to eat enough is something that Bill and Sharon had talked about ad infinitum. Was it Sharon's fault? His? Did they not sufficiently nourish her, not just in the obvious sense but emotionally as well? Was she unaware that she could suffer prematurely brittle bones or even a heart attack? Doubtful. Jill was anything but uninformed.

"Hi, Daddy," she says, tucking the earbuds into her pocket and turning off the machine.

"Darling," he says.

"Nice day, don't you think?" She smiles, broadly, and indicates their surroundings with a wave of her hand, as if perhaps she were a tour guide, or that the two of them had only just met.

It is a nice day, a glorious, even a perfect day: one of those perfect spring days that come along once or twice a season and sear into your senses like opium. Azaleas bloomed like cotton candy, tulips turned their red faces toward the sun, and in every direction parents watched young children or lovers embraced.

"Tommy told me that he talked to you," she says.

He nods, waiting for her to continue, which she does, almost immediately. "And the thing is, Dad, it's not like it was such a secret to begin with?"

"What do you mean?"

"Me and Natalie, we used to talk about it all the time. About the possibility, that is, that you may have had an affair."

"That's what you girls talked about?"

"Not literally all the time, Dad. Now and then. The way sisters talk to each other. You know?" But he doesn't know, not really, having been the youngest by many years in his own family, with sisters who were more like aunts to him, and cousins who seemed as strange and exotic as a flock of flamingos.

"And anyway, me and Natalie, we caught on to the fact that you were seeing someone else around the time that Mom started seeing that shrink. She used to talk about him all the time. What was his name? Dr. Berman?"

"Yes, that's right. Dr. Berman."

"And anyway, it just kind of added up: you weren't home, or when you were, you were distracted, and acted weird. You know you used to laugh all the time, even if what we were saying wasn't funny? Plus Mom was a wreck. I think she must have known about you for a while before she really knew, if you know what I mean. Because Mom? She wasn't stupid, you know."

"I know she wasn't, honey."

"So it's not like it came as this big, awful surprise, or anything, when she told us. I guess she just wanted to get everything off her chest. At the end, you know?"

At the very end they'd all been with her, witness to her last breath. As she had wanted. Practically from the moment she was diagnosed, she'd talked about how, when she died, she didn't want to be in a hospital, but at home, and how she wanted everyone to be with her, all of them, the only people who really meant anything.

"Actually, Dad," Jill now says. "I didn't ask you to meet me out here so we could talk about you and Mom."

"All right," Bill says.

"But before I say what I'm going to say, I want you to promise me one thing, okay?"

"I don't know. That depends on what it is."

"Okay. It's that I want you to promise me just to let me tell you in my own way, and not interrupt."

"I never interrupt."

"You're interrupting now. I want you just to listen, okay? And not offer advice, or help, or money, or anything. Do you think you can do that? Do you think you can just listen?"

God almighty, he wishes he had someone to talk to about all this! Had Sharon still been alive—but then again, none of these awkward, awful conversations would be taking place in the first place had Sharon not taken it upon herself to get every last little shred of her personal history out of her memory banks and into the next generation, where, no doubt, it would simmer and spread until it spilled over to others, and outward to the in-laws and the cousins and anyone who was willing to listen to family gossip.

"I'm going to have a baby," is what Jill finally says.

"You're going to have a baby." In the tumult of his worries about her health, it's all he manages to say.

"I told you not to interrupt."

But he can't help himself. "Who's the father, if I may ask?"

"Please, Daddy? Just let me tell you my way."

He nods, acquiescent.

"Okay, fine. The guy? I'd been dating him, not seriously. An okay-enough guy, is what I'm saying, but I'm not in love with him. I don't love him. Obviously the baby was a mistake, but now that I have it, I'm keeping it. Her."

"I take it the guy doesn't know?"

"It's just, well. I don't know quite how to say this, but I don't think I want to have a man in my life again. Not that way. Not permanently."

"But who—"

"Don't interrupt. It's true. I mean, after Richard"—her ex-husband—"and all that awfulness. And then there was that earlier time, in college." (What earlier time? Had he missed something?) "But basically, I just can't see it happening, ever. Because Dad—and this is something that Mom knew about, but you were oblivious, because, well the only way I can say it is that I think you were in denial. You didn't want to know what was happening in your own family, so you just looked the other way. But this thing with Tommy and all his bullshit? Because I want you to know, Tommy is so full of shit that words can't even describe how full of shit he is. Boo-hoo, poor Tommy, he has it so rough in that million-dollar condo, or however much it costs, and all those tough decisions he has to make between chardonnay and pinot noir. Dad, you're not going to like this, but the reason I have to tell you is that I've been angry with you for a very long time."

"You have?"

"Yes, because I could never tell you the truth. And well, now that Mom's gone, I was like: it's time. Because I don't want to be angry at you when you go to your grave. Not that you're going anywhere, I didn't mean it like that. It's more that, it's just that I have to tell you."

He feels like he's struggling to understand her words from under water, or like she's speaking a foreign language, or like he's suffering a small, barely perceptible stroke that has momentarily confused his ability to track linear meaning.

"Tommy has something to do with the baby?" he finally asks.

"No. Not exactly. And if you stop interrupting I can tell you. Whatever Tommy does or doesn't do now, fine, I wish him well. Him and Eleanor. But back then? When we were kids, Dad—" But she doesn't finish. Her eyes filling with tears, she stops in her tracks to wipe them away. "When we were kids, Tommy—well there's no other way to say it but to tell you the truth: he used to beat the crap out of me."

"What?"

"He hit me, Dad. A lot. You'd come home and tell us to stop squabbling and say things like 'boys will be boys,' but that wasn't what was going on. Tommy used to raise welts. And nobody stopped him!"

And now, rather than trying to control herself, she's sobbing, the wet sound coming from deep inside her, where, he supposes, the baby resides. Her face has gone from its usual palest of pale pinks to red, and her whole body is convulsing. "You never stopped him, Daddy!" she sobs. "Why didn't you ever stop him?"

Does this mean that he's permitted to talk? Because in fact he has plenty to say on the subject. For example, he'd like to point out that, while in general he was an indulgent parent, he never would have allowed any son of his to strike her. However, he doesn't say anything, because on top of his first thought comes a new and uncomfortable one: that he did in fact know that Tommy, as a boy, had hit his little sister. He'd told him to stop a thousand times, but at the same time, he'd never been particularly concerned. After all, siblings fought. All siblings, on occasion, hit each other. Didn't they?

"But Jill," he finally says. "Jilly, I did stop him, or at least I thought I did. As you know, I was at work an awful lot of the time—"

"Yeah," Jill says, blowing her nose. "At work or at some meeting or playing tennis."

"I admit I wasn't the best father in the world," he says. "And that I wasn't home a lot. But honey, your mother and I had a traditional marriage. She ran the house."

"She worked, too."

"That's true, but it was part-time, that was her choice, to work only part-time so she could be home when you three got back from school. That and, the way we figured it, she was the one who set the emotional tone of the house. I'm not saying we were right, or that we might not have been able to do it better. All I'm saying is that that's what we did, because that's what we thought was what we were supposed to do."

"But Daddy! He hit me! He hit me and hit me and hit me, and no one ever stopped him, and no one ever believed me! I was his punching bag, Daddy, and now, oh God! Now you see?"

But he doesn't see, not entirely. Tommy had hit his sister—and now, thirty years later, she stands here sobbing about it, and telling him that she's going to have a baby without having a husband, or even a boyfriend, to help her raise it. She's too thin. And on top of that he isn't allowed to help her.

Sharon would know what to do. Sharon would know what to say. Whereas what tumbles out of him is: "Darling, I'm glad you told me. But what can I do about it now? What do you want from me that might help?"

"Well, for one, you could be happy for me. About the baby, that is."

"I am happy, darling," Bill says. And maybe he even is. But mainly he's worried.

"Are you?"

He extends his arms, pulls his daughter to him. How delicate she is.
How birdlike her bones.

—

At the synagogue the usual crowd is gathered, nodding their heads in
unison as he dons his tallit and says the traditional blessings, before
adding one or two prayers of his own. Master of the Universe! I call
on You! I beseech You! Let me understand! But as usual the Master of
the Universe is silent, and all he hears is the rustling of old men as they
adjust their clothing and prepare to take their seats.

Over Sharon's protestations, he'd told her he'd say Kaddish for a
year, and even though she said it meant nothing to her—that he could
become a Buddhist monk for all she cared about that stuff—he intends
to keep that promise.

What else had he promised her, as she lay dying—dying and talking? He'd promised to divide her jewelry equally between their daughters, to watch over Jill, to make sure the children were what she called
"there for each other." To take care of his health. To get a cleaning lady.
But he hadn't promised anything regarding Clara. Clara Stein, who
still lived just over the township line. Had he?

—

Her house is exactly as he remembers it, with daffodils in the front
yard, and a dogwood tree, just beginning to bud. Even the color of the
shutters is the same dark gray, as are the colors and the shapes of the
curtains hanging in the living room windows. It is then that he sees a
flash, no more than an outline, really, through the mullioned glass of
the front door, and in an instant takes in the dark hair and brows, and
full red mouth, that he remembers. So: she is still beautiful. No doubt,
he thinks, she's always taken good care of herself—a woman like that!
With such pride! Such pride—and such fierce dignity! Suddenly, he is
filled with a wild, vibrant joy. He should have called her months ago.

He can see—or more precisely, sense her coming to the door, and opening it. And there she is, standing before him, an amused smile on her face, as if she never could forget the lovely joke that had been the two of them together. But when he lunges to embrace her, she puts her hands up, pushing him away. "No," she says. "I'm Isabel."

"I beg your pardon?"

"Clara's daughter."

"Ah," he says.

"Don't worry about it," she continues. "People do that all the time. I look so much like her."

He attempts a smile. He'd called just yesterday. Why hadn't Clara told him her daughter was visiting?

"I'm here with my children," she says. "Spending spring break with Nana."

"Of course," he says, and then, more awkwardly, "sorry."

"Don't worry about it," Clara's daughter repeats, flipping her head just slightly, so that her dark hair catches in the light, shimmering there like the surface of a lake, and so powerfully does she remind him of her mother, that for a moment, he lets himself believe that she is. He watches her, holding onto this illusion, when, another woman, this one deeply lined under a halo of silver curls, shuffles into the hallway.

"Well, look who it is!" she says as he catches his own reflection in the mirror, and sees, as if for the first time, how the years have left their markings on him, his insides, his outsides, his soul.

"Yes," he says. "It's me."

Mother

Though my father hated my mother, he reserved his greatest revulsion for my grandmother Annie. To get back at the two of them for what he considered to be, and in fact was, a coerced marriage, he slept with them both. His attraction to my mother was sufficient to produce me, and three years later, my sister. But fueled by rage and revulsion, his lust for my grandmother Annie knew no bounds.

Annie worked as a maid at a midtown hotel catering to well-heeled Orthodox Jews, a job that she felt to be far beneath her, especially as she had once been a well-heeled Orthodox Jew herself. Or so she said. It was impossible to know for sure, because while she most certainly was a Jew, it was all but impossible for me to envision her as anything other than what she was during the time that I knew her: chain-smoking, tough-talking, large-bosomed, and rough-skinned, with no regard for keeping the Sabbath and a disinclination to deprive herself of the abundance of the American table.

On weekends and holidays she wore flower-colored dresses with ropes of costume beads and painted her nails a bright, deep pink, and there she'd be, resplendent in her regal hues, sitting in our small front parlor, where in short breathless bursts she talked about the life she'd lived in England before her marriage.

Holding her teacup (it was always tea, never coffee) above her lap, she'd hold out her little finger before launching into the story I knew by heart. She'd been in one of the earliest Kindertransports, arriving in London in late 1938, only a few months before the Nazis killed her family.

Times were difficult and dark, but I never went to bed hungry, and on holidays we had the loveliest outings and rode the fattest ponies you've ever seen. My favorite was called Eloise.

Or she might say: all the girls wore clever, lovely hats to the synagogue, and we sat in our best frocks, giggling behind our hands.

Or: how I loved to dance the new dances coming from America.

You would have thought she'd been taken in by a family of come-down-in-the-world landowners or members of one of the higher orders of the bourgeoisie, when in fact the family that took her in, which to the day she died she considered to be her real family, had a cheese shop. During the war, when dairy was strictly rationed, they made a little extra by taking in laundry.

In any case, when Annie found herself pregnant by an American GI stationed in London after the war, she married him, moved with him to his parents' house in Baywater, and gave birth to my mother. When my mother was still very little, her GI father died, either from getting a chicken bone stuck in his esophagus or from slipping on black ice and falling into a coma—the accounts varied. Not long afterward, *his* father followed him into the grave, dying of a combination of grief and a diet heavy in salt and fat. That was Jewish cooking for you: meat and potatoes, highly salted and drowning in oil, and if you didn't eat it you were aiding and abetting the Nazis.

Annie and my mother continued living in Baywater with Annie's bereaved mother-in-law (my great-grandmother) in the comfortable apartment to which my American GI granddad had brought my pregnant grandmother. My mother remembered seeing *her* grandmother sitting on a pale-green sofa, crying, no doubt for the double loss of husband and son, and no doubt because, on top of everything else, she didn't much care for Annie.

Annie was difficult and ungrateful. She sat around the apartment complaining and refused to get a job to help offset expenses. My great-grandmother pointed out that she herself was too old to go out looking for a job, and in any case it was her apartment, the least Annie could do was help out with the bills. She further declared that she was more than capable of looking after her sole grandchild while Annie was at work. Annie said that not in a million years would she leave her precious daughter with an old bat. Back and forth they went. Their fights grew so loud that neighbors heard them.

Despite her temper, Annie wasn't alone. She had girlfriends with whom she played cards. There may have also been a man or two. But that may only be rumor. That may only be wishful or wistful thinking. My own mother only knew that Annie liked to get her way, which included fighting with her mother-in-law until things came to a boil and she was told to either get a job or get out.

Annie and my mother moved in with some distant cousins in Brooklyn, and then with a man named Larry who worked delivering air-conditioning units to houses in Long Island, and finally to a room on the basement-level of a house in North Woodmere, where Annie worked as a live-in housekeeper for a family of well-off first-generation Jews.

After my upbringing in England, she'd say, it was a big plunge down in the world, I can't deny it. The Jews I worked for . . . Russian? Romanian? They didn't say. Chattering on with those awful accents of theirs. Books everywhere. Dust. And I was supposed to keep the house clean as a bone. Two bigger slobs you'd never seen, and their kids were even worse. Then the oldest son—he was in college—took a shine to me. Flirting with me, making suggestions. Which is when I said, okay, enough, no more!

By the time she was telling me her stories, Annie was one of those indistinctly baggy women who are almost impossible to imagine as either young or pretty. Her legs seemed to be of such determined heft that they appeared to have grown straight from the earth. As for her breasts, they seemed as sturdy and fibrous as cushions. I remember being five, six, seven, and I couldn't for the life of me figure out where you would put such accoutrements, or what you'd do with them once you figured it out. Had the young man whose parents she'd worked for been entranced by the size of her bosom? Had he even existed?

During Annie's visits our father absented himself. He was absent so often that it's hard to say if he made a special point of being away when he knew that Annie would be visiting, or if he merely wasn't home because he was rarely home if he could help it. Either way he wasn't there, leaving me free to sit on Annie's lap and play with the heavy costume beads she wore around her neck. Sometimes she'd bring me a present: a book about kittens, a puzzle, a pencil with a red, yellow, and green tip, all combined.

We lived in southern Queens, close enough to JFK that the incessant ascending and descending airplanes went unremarked. Our house backed onto a large brick apartment building, which blocked the light, but otherwise it wasn't a bad house. It wasn't a good house, either. It was a red-brick bungalow reached by four red-brick steps, its interior clad from top to bottom in dark wood paneling, and its plain front facing the street. My mother put floral-pattern curtains in the bedrooms and bright-blue wall-to-wall carpeting downstairs, where the living room was connected to what she called the dining room by an open archway, behind which was the kitchen. Upstairs: three bedrooms and a bathroom. Downstairs, as described. There was a small basement, too, where my father, typical of his generation, set up a workbench. The workbench, however sacred to my father's sense of himself as an American, was little more than a single, rickety shelf where screwdrivers, hammers, and a jumble of nails, screws, bolts, nuts, wire, thumbtacks, and mice droppings mingled together in a shoebox. Under this shelf, lightbulbs were stored along with some crusted-over, disused sponges. My father only went down there when he wanted to drink in private.

It wasn't as if he couldn't fix things though. In fact, he could fix almost anything. But he had no use for his skills, at least not when he was at home. It was during the day, when he was at work, that his hands came alive. He worked for the MTA as an engineer, which meant that he was the guy they literally sent down to the tracks to fix them when things went awry. There he had friends, camaraderie, a sense of accomplishment. But by the time he came home he'd already be drunk, reeking of booze and grease. He'd take a shower (or not), fight with my mother (or not), hit her (or not), and pass out upstairs in the queen-sized bed with its nubby green bedspread. He rarely drank enough to throw up in bed, but when he did, my mother went at him for days about how she'd had to scrimp and save in order to buy that lovely green bedspread.

Technically, our house had three bedrooms. But my own room, at the top of the stairs, was barely big enough to fit more than my single bed, and I did my homework at the kitchen table. My sister, though my junior, had the slightly larger room. The master bedroom, with two windows, faced the street. To this day I can remember the sound of every footfall on the stairs, the closed-in smell of the well-worn carpeting and how, in the summer, even with the windows wide open, there was an unpleasant odor, unconnected to cleanliness or the lack of—my mother was a wizard with the mop, a serial-vacuum-cleaner, and a compulsive wiper-offer of furniture, countertops, and floors— but rather coming from our bodies themselves. The smell of anxiety as it pours out of pores. The whiff of fear. The crush of boredom. The shame of having hope.

Despite whatever copious amount of his salary my father pissed away, my mother managed to scrabble enough away not only to keep up appearances but also to send both me and my sister to a nearby Jewish school. The Abraham Hebrew Academy was by no means a good school, nor did it provide much in the way of a rigorous Jewish education. But it did provide something that was important to my mother, namely that the other Jewish families in the neighborhood sent their kids there, and the cousins who'd briefly taken her and Annie in, when Annie's mother-in-law had at last kicked them out of the apartment in Baywater, insisted that a Jewish school was the only way to ensure that American children remain Jewish. This was something that my mother hadn't given a fig about until, upon marrying my cynical, secular Ukrainian-Soviet Jewish father, she did. My father spoke Ukrainian, Russian, a smattering of Yiddish, and, in time, English, which he peppered with Irish locutions—lads, *reet you are, oul wan*, what's the *craik*?—that he picked up from the Irish cops who regularly didn't ticket him for drunk driving and the Irish workers who made up the bulk of the TWU local to which he belonged. He liked them; they liked him. They didn't mind that he was a Jew. In fact, it seems that they gave him a special rank among them, as their own honorary Christ killer. It was a joke. No one believed in Christ. What they believed in was getting on with things, drinking, sports, and putting the trauma of their parents' and grandparents' and great-grandparents' generations behind them. All of them had trauma back then. Every single one of them. No one talked about it. How could they? Trauma as a concept hadn't yet been invented.

The point is: despite my father's multilingualism, ability to fix things, and robust sense of humor, as far as my mother was concerned, he was a piece of shit.

He had had three years of high school at a technological institute, and another three years of off-and-on training at a pay-as-you-go vocational school in Brooklyn that the Chabad Lubavitch who'd arranged for his immigration to America sent him to. Still, he remained determinedly agnostic, claiming that God was no more than a myth, and Judaism no more than a story. He'd merely done what he'd had to do to convince the Lubavitch Jews who had found him at his Kiev technological institute that he was grateful for their help, and more to the point, willing. The Soviets had stamped out the Faith of Our Fathers. So what? On American soil, he would rejoice in it!

Or so he would tell us. Made jocular by just the right amount of drink, he'd narrate the story of his fake conversion (fake to him, not to his sponsors) in his Irish-American-Russian-Ukrainian accent while my mother rolled her eyes and my sister and I would try to hide our giggles.

—

They'd met at a Chabad-sponsored singles event that my mother had attended to meet men, and my father had attended to get free food. Though by then he'd been in America for over three years, he was still hungry, not just for food, but also for some sense of comfort, some sense of home, of belonging to something. When my mother took him back to the apartment she shared with three other girls near City College (my mother may have been crazy but she wasn't dumb) neither of them were thinking that a child would be the result. Hence the rushed—and for my father, coerced—marriage. Hence my father's lifelong hatred for Annie, who had threatened to report him to the authorities if he didn't make my mother what she called "an honest woman." It was an empty threat, of course. Though abortion wasn't yet legal in New York, my mother could have easily found a way to have one. Also, there were no authorities. But my father, who'd spent the first twenty-one years of his life in the Soviet Union, didn't know that.

They were married a week later. It was a religious service, conducted by the same Chabad Lubavitch rabbi who'd helped my father leave Kiev and, later, would counsel my mother to have patience and me to study child development at Stern College for Women in order to be a kindergarten or first-grade teacher.

—

I was just beginning to realize that the education I was receiving at the Abraham Hebrew Academy was subpar when my father came home one night and punched my mother so hard that she vomited. She fled to the bathroom and slammed the door behind her, but he caught up, kicked her, and when she fell face-first onto the closed toilet seat, began to strangle her as well. While she screamed and he yelled, my sister and I pulled him off her, turned her over, and began patting her face with a wet washcloth. A minute later, we heard the front door slam.

The trouble had started earlier that day, when Annie had shown up at the house with a bag full of my father's dirty socks and under-wear, saying that it wasn't her job to wash his things, and when my mother just stood there gawping, Annie added that my father wasn't all that good in bed anyway. When my mother finally understood what her mother was saying, she pushed Annie so hard that she fell against the stove, causing a slow bleed in her brain. By the time it was caught, the damage had been done. She never worked again. I don't know what she lived off, either, because after that, she disappeared so entirely from our lives it was as if I'd dreamed her.

My father vanished from our lives also, though not entirely. First he came back to pick up his stuff, and after that to take the TV set. Once he came by to wish my sister a happy birthday. And as the years rolled on, he'd occasionally show up to take us out for pizza or a day at the beach, but by then he was a stranger. Before that, he'd been a monster, a terrible and terrifying force of nature, but not a stranger. Now he was, and though our house quieted down, I missed him. My mother did not. She did, however, refuse to give him a divorce.

She figured that she'd get more money out of him if he was still legally tied to her, and honest to God, she may well have been right, because my mother, in all her bitterness, remained in that small house under the flight paths of jumbo jets, where she continued to put three meals on the table, hector us about our grades, refuse to buy retail, and complain. In other words, other than the near complete absence of my father, things continued on exactly as before.

Except for one thing, that is. With my father gone, my mother doubled down on holiness. She cut her hair short, wore a wig, obsessed over separating milk and meat, and whenever she was angry or disturbed or wanted to make a point, muttered one of the handful of Hebrew prayers she knew. She had taken up the mantle of Orthodox Judaism far too late in life to know her way around the liturgy, and though she might have studied and learned, becoming conversant and comfortable within the tradition, she didn't. She was either too lazy, too stubborn, too unmoored, or too consumed with victimhood to bother. Either way, becoming devout animated her and made her more determined than ever to assert her will, including that her two daughters also become religious. To that end, I was to transfer from Abraham Hebrew to an Orthodox all-girls school on the eastern shore of Long Island. I would have to take two busses to get there, and wear nothing other than heavy dark skirts and long-sleeved shirts. It wasn't a question of how I would manage, but rather, a question of how I would resist. But resist I did, and when I told my mother that if she made me go there I'd find Annie and live with her, she slapped me.

"You're already a lazy slug. Do you want to be a whore as well?"

What I wanted was an education. Externally, the Abraham Hebrew Academy was run by teachers whose own education struck me even then as woefully superficial; internally it was ruled by a handful of horrific girls who all went to the same summer camp in the Catskills and a cohort of boys with relatives in Israel who liked to talk about which elite IDF military unit they wanted to join when they turned eighteen. I was so bored there that I could feel my synapses shrinking. I'd been miserable there from the get-go, but as the years went on, I became the butt of jokes, too. Then my father left and I came upon a solution that would solve all my problems: my solution was to stop attending school completely. I'd wander around the neighborhood, take the train to the city, go to the library. Eventually I was absent so much that the school kicked me out, and my mother had no choice but to enroll me at JFK High. After school, I shut myself up in my tiny room and read.

—

I tried to love her—even then, I tried to love her—but my heart was entangled in barbed wire. I grew up nonetheless. Every now and then I'd pick up the phone and call her, but Mother rarely wanted to talk, and when she did, it was only to complain. Was she proud of my accomplishments? She never said so. And then she died. Heart failure. She was only sixty-three, and as the eldest—and the only one of the two of us who lived nearby—it fell to me to return to the house to get it ready for sale.

I hadn't been home in nearly twenty years, and worried that the house would be packed to the gills with decrepit junk, that I'd find the lair of a hoarder, or worse. Instead it was almost exactly as it had been, clumsy with oversized furniture, Judaica, and knick-knacks, but spotless, smelling of a mixture of cleaning fluids, newly vacuumed rugs, and a lack of sunlight and air. It was my job to sort through her things, get rid of the clutter, give away that which neither my sister nor I wanted, and throw everything else out. So it wasn't until the third day there that I started in on the second floor, where I unearthed a large, sealed cardboard box marked clearly with my name. Inside it, I found a record of my childhood: thirteen years of report cards, various school projects, letters I'd written home from my one summer at summer camp in eastern Long Island, Mother's and Father's Day cards made of construction paper, crayon drawings, my bat mitzvah certificate, photographs, and a stapled-together collection of haiku that I'd written in the fourth grade.

On the silver tree
Outside my small window
Night is coming in.

The Dick

At first June only had glimmerings, a whiff of something slightly ugly, but she tamped it down, didn't pay attention, not to that first phone call, which, after all, she herself had placed. She and her husband, Don, were putting up a fence for their dogs, and would that be okay? Of course it was okay, Bob Lesterfield said in his heavy Jersey accent, so heavy, so long in the vowels, so guttural in its undertones, that it was as if he were doing an impression of someone doing an impression of a Jersey tough: an audition for *The Sopranos*. It was her property, wasn't it? Well yes: she and Don had only just bought it, intending to use it primarily as a summerhouse, but they wanted to be good neighbors, they didn't want their dogs to be bothersome: they were big dogs, loud, bred to work—the husky to pull a sled, the Aussie to herd sheep. Nah, don't worry about it, Bob Lesterfield said, adding that there wouldn't be any trouble between them, not on his end anyway, just so long as she understood that he had a right-of-way to the semi-shared semi-circular driveway that swooped up the steep embankment where both houses now stood, because, he went on, let me tell you, the people you bought your house from—the Safers?—they were wonderful, the nicest people in the world, he never had any trouble from them, not in fifteen years, but the people before them: they were the neighbors from hell. That's what he called them. The neighbors from hell, had no common sense, broke up the driveway with their big truck, and worse, this one time . . .

And he was off and going. She tried to keep track of all the ins and all the outs, all the characters, all the twists and turns in the plot, the various motifs, but in the end it all came to this: the neighbor from hell was using his sanding machine on the porch, at eleven at night, it was making a racket, the neighbor from hell had no common sense, so he, Bob Lesterfield, had to come over with a baseball bat and smash the machine.

"It was the only way I could get the neighbor from hell's attention," said Bob Lesterfield, before launching into another long story, this one about the elderly sister of the original owner, the man who'd built the house that June and her husband had just bought, a prosperous businessman, in Utica, he owned hardware stores, built the original house and then the boathouse and then a kind of grotto where his family would have picnics—never dreaming of course that one day his estate would be carved up into smaller lots and only the original house, your house now I guess, intact as it was back then—but anyway, she died, this elderly aunt, and she had loved roses, she'd kept rose gardens up there, up there where your toolshed is, that used to be a rose garden, and let me tell you, when she died, they say, and she died right there in the little bedroom in back, the one with the rose-petaled wallpaper, when she died the whole house was filled with the smell of crushed rose petals, rose petals after the rain . . .

"You don't believe me, do you?" said Bob Lesterfield over the phone.

"I do believe you," June said.

"You and me," he said. "We're gonna get along fine."

"He talked an awful lot," she reported to Don over dinner. It was October. The house had been theirs for approximately two weeks, but she wanted to get the fence in before the hard frost made it impossible. "I couldn't follow it all, but it seems like he's been there a while, he knows all the neighbors, everyone's backstory."

"As long as I don't have to deal with him," Don said. Don didn't like talky neighbors. He didn't like talky people in general. He himself was reserved, almost taciturn, prone to storms of anxiety that nearly shut him down—shutting him off, sealing him inside himself—entirely.

"Don't worry about it," she said. "It'll be fine."

But it wasn't fine. It wasn't fine at all, although in retrospect the main thing that seemed out of joint, so not-right that she wanted to scream, was her own response, or rather lack of response, or rather, *poorly rendered* response: her tender overtures, her ass-licking, her capitulation, whatever you wanted to call it, it was cringe-inducing and awful. Because what happened next was that he came over.

He didn't even knock but rather, on that first full week of summer, the first week that the black flies were diminished enough to make life on the lake tolerable if not yet attractive, he popped his head into the top part of the double Dutch door—that huge wide plank of a door that convinced her that she and Don needed to buy the house even before she'd seen the rest of it—and, seeing the painter she'd hired to replace the sainted Safers' depressing fern- and moss- and frog-greens with a bath of pure white, announced his presence and let himself in. She'd liked the painter right away. Even on the phone, she'd liked him. He had a warm voice and had called her right back. Now he was up on a ladder and June was sitting on the sofa, her laptop open on her lap, sending emails. She was always doing that: sending emails, putting her words out into the email-sphere in a never-ending hope that somewhere, somehow, they'd land. She was a professor in the English department at Sarah Lawrence, an impressive position, an enviable one even, but she was dying to get out of there, to go someplace where her students might actually want to know something about how literature is made, what its guts are, how it lives, rather than what they seemed to want at Sarah Lawrence, which was an argument for the oppression of whatever subgroup the particular student belonged to, or, barring political point-making, an inside track to becoming writers themselves. And not just writers, but creative writers: the next generation of Hemingways and Bellows and Styrons and Baldwins and Faulkners, only forget about it, they didn't read the patriarchy. Her specialty was the modern Hebrew novel, another dead-ender, this literature of hope and despair written in a revivified language that only a few million people understood, and no one outside Israel cared about other than a handful of critics and academics.

Those who can't do, teach, and there it is, her life story, in a maxim. But teach she could, and did, and does—but it isn't working anymore, not at Sarah Lawrence, not even with the tenure she'd gotten two decades ago followed by the various honors and invitations and grants, and she wanted out, and more to the point, she wanted up. She wanted Columbia; she wanted NYU; she wanted Princeton or Yale. Even some of the SUNYs might be better, she'd speculate, but it was all so much speculation, because no matter how often she schmoozed or how many conferences she attended and books she herself wrote— *Naked in Galicia: Humor and Pathos in Ottoman Palestine, The High Priest of Jerusalem, The Dancing Jew on the Dancing Fricative: How the Hebrew Bible Birthed Black Humor*—so far it was the same thing, over and over: there was no room for her, no need, no appointment, no opening, and why, her friends and family and, most of all, her husband, Don, would ask, would she want to leave Sarah Lawrence to begin with? She was at *Sarah Lawrence* for God's sake. A cushier landing did not exist, not on God's green earth, and not on God's other green places, either. She knew that, and yet wasn't satisfied.

"You ever work with fella named Dick Hinton?" Bob Lesterfield asked the painter, the nice man—she was sure he was a nice man, the kind of man you could trust—as if she herself were a bystander, or an afterthought. It hadn't been easy to find him, either, this pleasant, soft-spoken man whom she'd found by calling every hardware store within fifty miles of the lake to ask for the names and numbers of reputable painters until finally, here he was, up on a ladder, considering the presence of Bob Lesterfield below.

"Come on in, Bob," she said from the corner in the living room where she'd been tapping somewhat nonproductively into her laptop for the better part of the afternoon—a deadline, she told herself, though it wasn't true. More like an *internal deadline*. More like *better to work than to be swallowed up by that nameless thing, that anxiety, that dysregulation, that surge and storm of panic that—that . . .*

The irony was lost on him, though, and she was hit by a small electrical storm of unpleasantness that traveled twice up her spine before exploding somewhere in the lower regions of her brain.

Ping!

She was nothing if not self-aware, and yet all the self-awareness in the world did little to tamp down the twists of tweaky discomfort that flitted through her as she observed Bob Lesterfield step into the open expanse where she planned to put a piano, the place where, when she and Don had seen the house a year ago, the former owner, the husband, had displayed hand-built furnishings, in the classic Adirondack style: a birch wood chair, an elaborate bench, an even more elaborate cabinet, and above it, a large map of the mountains. Apparently, he'd been an avid mountaineer—and now was retiring, selling the house, leaving the lake and the mountains and the storms that blew in from the west, turning the placid blue waters where people boated and waterskied into black whips of froth and foam.

"Because let me tell you something, see, the way it is—with him— Dick Hinton?" Bob Lesterfield said. "Take it from me, the guy, well, I don't want to speak ill of the dead . . ." and he was off and running. June both did and did not pay attention to what he was saying. Shop talk: planks, drill bits.

Bob Lesterfield went on and on: "People can be so stupid, so stupid, I tell you, stupid, what I call stupid, is doing the same stupid thing over and over, and not learning, is that stupid or what?"

"People will be people, for sure," the other one, the nice man with the gray hair and closely kept beard, replied as she sat in her own living room as if she didn't exist, or, worse, as if it weren't her own living room at all, as if she were there by permission of Bob Lesterfield.

Who was spreading his legs further and further apart, and he was a short man, not much taller than she was, but his legs, they spread and spread, he was a colossus spreading out in her living room.

Their living room. The former owners—the Safers—(in his pronunciation, *Savers*) the best people ever, is who they were. He was a doctor, a surgeon, a Jewish surgeon, can you believe that, a Jewish surgeon, with his fancy white hands, but he could build anything, look at that furniture he built, and if I needed a hand, with anything, and I mean anything, all I had to do was ask, he'd help.

I'm Jewish, she said to herself as she sat, not typing, listening to the sound of Don's feet from upstairs, and then, a moment later, his appearance.

"You must be the husband," said Bob Lesterfield, not moving, his feet planted.

"Don," Don said, nodding, as he did, to indicate a polite hello.

"Donald Louis Greenstein, to be precise," Bob Lesterfield said, and then when Don said nothing, he continued with: "I know all about you, my friend, don't think I don't, I've got the goods, you're all over the internet."

Don shifted his weight slightly.

"But don't worry about it. I don't have any trouble with liars-for-hire. My own son, my oldest, he went to Seton Hall law, got himself a nice little gold mine, he's down in Cape May County."

"I'm not a lawyer," Don said.

"Hey," Bob Lesterfield said. "It's okay with me, what you are. I'm not prejudiced."

"I'm glad to hear it."

"Why, you think I'm prejudiced?"

"I don't know you," Don said. Then he made that same little bobbing motion with his head again, excused himself, and went back upstairs.

"The nicest, they were the nicest, the Safers, the best neighbors you could ask for, even with those soft hands, did I tell you? Didn't matter if you were Irish-English-whatever, like me, or a Pakistani from Pakistan or a South Sea islander, they didn't care, didn't go in for stuff like that."

He turned to the man on the ladder.

"And let me ask you, while you're here, let me ask you something. Because you've been working these parts, doing carpentry, construction, whatever comes your way, something like that, am I right?"

"That's right."

"Been at it for a while?"

"A number of years."

"Ever worked with a fella named Bucky Mc' something? Wife's name was Brenda, Barbara, something like that, they'd work together, those two."

"Can't say I have."

"Because the husband—Bucky—he was—but she was—she was, the wife—she was—almost a man, she was so strong, and if you ever saw her with a chainsaw? A woman with a chainsaw, that was something to see, am I right?"

June checked her emails. She wrote to both her sons, asking them if they'd consider coming, anytime really, to spend some time with them on the lake, they could swim, canoe, go hiking.

"It's so beautiful here," she wrote.

"So yeah," Bob Lesterfield said from astride the wooden floor, his glance falling at last on her, in her chair in the corner, looking surprised to find her there. "I tell you, the best carpenter I ever worked with, hands-down, was my own old man. The old man—" And here tears welled up in his eyes. "Look what can I say? I'm selfish. I am. My father died at seventy-nine, and people told me, they said, you had him a long time, he lived a good life. But me, I didn't have enough of him. I wanted more of him. Nursed him until the day he died. People said: Bob, you took care of him, you did good by him. But I would have taken twenty more years of cleaning him up, changing his drains, spoon-feeding him—you name it—over not having him. Like I said, I'm selfish."

"You never stop missing them," June said, ridiculously, so eager she was to join the conversation, to stand up and be counted. "They die, but the grieving never really stops."

"You know what? That's very true."

"What did he want?" Don said, later, when he emerged back into the living room from the space she'd had carved out for him, carved out of what had once been a rather amorphous non-space under the eaves, where the former owners—the marvelous Safers—had kept their water-skiing equipment. He'd been working there for most of the afternoon. He too was an academic, in his case, a professor of law. That's how they'd met: through the academic grapevine, although in their case it had been an unusual meeting, his having been at a law conference on the same weekend that she was at a conference on Hebrew language literature in, of all places, Berlin. They were the only two Americans there. They went out for a beer and traded Holocaust jokes:

What does the Nazi say to the Black Jew?
Get to the back of the gas chamber.

"He just wanted to schmooze," she told him now. "He's harmless, Don. He talks too much, but he's harmless."

"He was creepy, the way he said he'd googled me. The guy's a creep."

"He said you were all over the internet, which is true, you are, and anyway, I think he just—he just talks a lot."

"If you say so," Don said before drifting back up, where he had a view of the lake, and was happy.

—

She'd bought the house—correction, *they'd* bought the house—as a kind of celebratory statement, after it turned out that the cancer that was supposed to kill Don not only didn't kill him but went away entirely. When they broke the good news to him, Don's doctors told him to get on with his life.

"Just don't go near any killer whales," his oncologist had joked.

"Will do."

Tears of joy and relief, and a bottle of champagne later, he and June decided, what the hell, it was now or never, life was to be enjoyed, why don't they finally go looking for the summerhouse they'd been talking about looking for ever since the boys had gone off to college? The place where their sons, now grown, could bring their future wives, their future children and dogs and minivans. A summer home. Their own dacha. The first thing she'd done, after taking possession of it, was rip down the drapes that had covered the house's old, elegant windows. Let the sun shine in! And as for neighbors—what neighbors?

Oh yeah. Bob. Bob Lesterfield, on the other side of the fence she'd had built for the dogs—because, no, she could never leave the dogs behind, the whole point of a summer home was that it would be for the whole family, dogs included, a place for all of them to work and swim and read long novels on the porch at twilight—and in any event, Bob Lesterfield's semi-log house, up the hill and behind a line of pines, was nowhere near her windows.

"Please come and spend time here," she wrote again to both boys. "It's your house too." But it wasn't. In some profound way, where words didn't reach, it was hers, and hers alone. Her vision. Her refuge. A deep seated hope, a hope based on faith, that in this house, in this place, she and Don might carry on, that despite their disappointments and the bitterness that had flared up between them as early as Berlin—when he'd insisted that no American, no matter how precise her Hebrew, could possibly be as sensitive to the nuances of Hebrew literature as a native speaker—they might find that peaceful pond again, the pond in which they'd both lain, after sex, in their early years together.

There was crap in the house. All kinds of crap, from God alone knew how many generations and how many different families who'd spent their summers there, leaving behind, with each parting, almost-finished bottles of sunscreen, squares of leftover fabric, long-disused pillows, picnic paraphernalia, discarded bits of wiring, disused plumbing, last year's bestsellers from the Book of the Month Club, brightly flowered hand towels long since faded into various shades of sand, scraps of wood, bags of straw, rusted-over tools, dead fans. She'd paid a local man to haul it all away for her, another thousand dollars gone, no pain no gain, her late father had left her with more than enough but to this day she would have preferred his approval to any amount of money.

It had been for his approval that she'd striven so hard, studying and then studying some more to prove to her wealthy father and his entire cool and disapproving family that she wasn't a dull-witted thing, disappointingly average, a chip that hadn't fallen anywhere near the old block but rather some aberration. And she'd done it, too, drawn on and further on by the miraculous fact that the Jews continued to refuse to disappear, and, along the way, kept writing about it.

—

A day passed. Two. The weather was terrible, either raining and cold inside, or muggy and filled with bugs. Don, in his haven under the eaves, didn't seem to notice. He was happy, productive, content. June strained. She strained to write. She strained to make coherent what wasn't. She strained to master the panic that kept rising in her throat like a spiritual flu.

Then the better-behaved of their two poorly behaved dogs, Bluster, the big rambling part-Aussie part-who-knew-what, the headstrong piece of fur and slobber that they'd raised from a puppy and who, at

night, routinely got in bed with them for a good long snuggle before
he was sent to his official sleeping corner in the basement: he barked.
He planted himself in the corner of the enclosed field behind the house
and barked at Bob Lesterfield as he was sitting on his porch, eating
breakfast. June could hear the barking from the kitchen, where she
was gazing out the window over the sink, doing dishes. She was thinking about how lovely the wildflowers were, the spots of yellow that
resembled buttercups but weren't, the drifts of Queen Anne's lace,
the lady's slipper, the sheep laurel, all of it so lovely, so quiet and right,
when there was a tapping on the window behind her and there he
was, her neighbor, Bob Lesterfield, and he didn't wait for her to dry
off her hands or take off her apron before, through the screen, he told
her that her fucking dog was a fucking menace and he wouldn't fucking
put up with any fucking insanity, not in the woods, not at his country
place, that he'd built from the studs up with his late father, the father
whom he'd nursed through his last illnesses, oh no, and she was going
to be sorry if she thought that just because she was a college graduate and apparently she and Don were people of some means—that's
how he put it, "some means,"—it wasn't going to fucking work if she
thought she could just let her fucking wolves run around the fucking
property barking like that.

"What?" she said.

"You fucking heard me," he said, tromping off, but not before adding that if she fucking wanted a war, he'd give her one.

"What was that?" said Don, coming downstairs from his own work,
at his own laptop, in the place under the eaves that she'd hired a carpenter to make into an office for him: a long desk, spanning the entire
width of the room, which she'd painted white herself. The bookshelves,
thick and wide and tall enough to accommodate the thick legal tomes
he needed for his own next book, his own next project—this time he
was working on something to do with refugees and rape, despite her
own profession she could never quite keep track of all the subtleties at

war within her husband's mind . . . the Talmudic turnings, the thinking within the thinking.

"Nothing."

"I heard shouting."

"Our neighbor," she said, her voice trembling. "Apparently he doesn't like our dogs."

"I told you," Don said. "There's something not-okay about that guy."

"He's fine, Don," she said. "Let me handle this, okay? I'll handle it."

"I don't think you should handle it."

"I don't think you should handle it, either," she said.

"Do you agree?" she said when he didn't answer.

"I told you," he finally said. "When he told me that he'd googled me?"

"So what," she said. "Don't you google people?"

"That's not the point," he said. "The point is how he insinuated that he knew all about me."

"If he googled you, he probably does know all about you."

"Don't go over there, June," Don said. "He's a loose cannon. I'm telling you, he is."

But Don didn't like confrontation. Never had. That was one reason why, early on in his legal career, he'd left the law firm in Boston where they were paying him boatloads of money and sending him regularly to London, for a career as a teacher. As a professor, first at Rutgers, and then, when it came open to him, at Cardozo. Where he was satisfied.

The person who wasn't satisfied was June. Why *not* Yale, why *not* Hopkins or Penn? Her work was as good—was better—than anyone's. It was. She knew it. And she didn't know it in the way that she was hoping to convince herself that it was, but because it was. She was a reader. She knew good work when she saw it. And she knew it when that good work, when those important words, came out of her own hands, came from somewhere above her head and into her spine and then down through her arms where they came out, on the page, through her tapping, moving fingers. Her fingertips. Her beautiful, sensitive fingertips.

Because that's the way she'd lit on, all those years and dreams ago, when no matter what she did or how she dressed or even how well she eventually did in school didn't seem to make a dent: not in her feelings about herself, not in the way that her father and her father's large family—the only side of the family that counted as her mother's side was stunted, small, barely even a family at all, a race of people who tended to die before old age, and, along the way, only tentatively made babies, and then only in small numbers—saw her. She knew because they told her so.

They said: June, you don't have to go to college if you don't want to, you know, you might think of doing something else entirely, or you could go to junior college, see if you like it. They said: You take after your mother's side of the family (in the family context, a profound insult, as her mother's side of the family, their numbers small, tended toward small-bore careers, in insignificant, small cities: Albany, Syracuse, Wilmington). They said: Nice house, ha-ha, leaving the bitter part, the ugly part, unsaid, and therefore all the more painful. Aunts and uncles. Cousins. Her own older sister. Even now, in her fifties, June can't fathom what they might have been thinking, or why any one of them would have been so consistently cruel. Even now, sitting and typing away, on the ninth chapter of her new book (tentatively entitled *Fuck You in Hebrew: A Primer in Survival*, but not really, she'd never get away with it) she wants to call them all, including aunts and uncles long disappeared into dementia, and say:

In high school, I was a straight A student.
But I could never take standardized tests.
Nice house—

Nice house, ha, if only, this house, this paradise . . . She hung up her apron, put on her sandals, and crossed the piney expanse of what had once been the estate—now divvied up, allowing Bob Lesterfield to construct his semi-log house on the perch above the rise where she'd built a fenced enclosure for the dogs—and knocked.

"Go the fuck away."

"For God's sake," she said. "Why don't we talk about this?"

He opened the door a crack. Behind him, she saw a woman with dyed black hair surrounding an oval face slightly crumpled into itself with age, but pleasant enough, neither vacant nor afraid nor empathetic nor either intelligent or unintelligent.

"Then let me talk to your wife. Mrs. Lesterfield? Daphne?" she said, knowing that it was Daphne, and moreover, that Daphne's name was Daphne, because Bob had told her, and moreover, who else could the woman with the dyed black hair be?

"You ain't talking to my wife," said Bob Lesterfield, coming forward from inside the deep gloom of what she thought was his living room but couldn't quite tell—leather sofa, large TV, a couple of folding chairs and more tools than she'd ever seen outside a hardware store—"Talk to me if you have to, but then, we need to come to some agreement, you and me, because, my friend, I don't take kindly to that kind of noise."

So they talked. Or rather, he talked. He talked, and she danced. She danced right, she danced left, she danced around his words, his egotism, his threatening chest-puffed assertions, and in the end she agreed to get a bark-reducing collar, actually, no, she'd never even heard of one, but she'd look into it, immediately she'd look into it, and then he told her about how he'd nursed his father through his last years, as he was dying of emphysema, and how he'd do anything just to get one day with his dad back, he and his dad, together, they'd built this place—he indicated the front porch where she was now sitting in a low chair that hurt her back—and she matched his story with one of her own, the story of how Don had been dying of cancer at the same time that her father was dying of heart disease, only she fibbed, because Don hadn't died, and her father had, and not only that, but her father had died a full fifteen years before Don's CAT scan had come back with spots on it showing lesions on his liver. Then, thinking about her father—the distant father who'd left her with more money than she knew what to do with and who, well before he died, piled her with books that he thought she'd like, hunting them down in used-book stores and weird corners of Jerusalem and Tel Aviv, always with the same inscription—because you love stories, daughter—she burst into tears.

"There, there," Bob Lesterfield said. "Look, it's okay, okay? We got a deal now. You and me, we're going to be friends."

Were they? Were they ever going to be friends? She slunk back over across the driveway and told Don that she deserved a Nobel Peace Prize and he said, okay, good for you, I can't deal with that asshole, more power to you, and everything was okay, sort of not really, because by the time she was hauling down New York 87 her guts were in a twist and she could barely contain her sphincter muscles until she got to the ladies' room at the Target in Queensbury, where she searched the pet aisle in vain for anything resembling a bark-reducing collar, and then had to go on to the PetSmart, where she bought one for $43.40 and nearly burst into tears when the young man who was helping her assured her that they'd had enormous success with the collars, so much so that if it didn't work she could bring it back, used, and he'd refund her—and such kindness and decency got to her, made her sad and grateful and desperate for reassurance—and then she was back in the car and headed back to her house—her house, not the Safers'—and the next morning, she put the collar on Bluster, apologizing to him the whole time, poor dear Bluster, she didn't want to hurt him, it didn't chafe his neck, his throat, did it? And kissing his head and then the sweet spot between his eyes she sent him back outside, praying, praying...

But two days later it was their other dog, the husky, the one whose yip had never deepened, who literally jumped around chasing her tail, who was the culprit. She'd taken Bluster on a walk, and when she returned, Sadie was at the gate, howling, and Bob Lesterfield was sitting on her front porch, smoking a cigar.

"We have a little problem, my friend," he said. "Where's your husband?"

She didn't know. All she knew was that Don wasn't upstairs in his haven under the rafters. Was he swimming? Had he gone on a jog?

"I don't know."

"That's unfortunate."

"He's probably gone on a run."

"He shouldn't do that. Not with your wolf howling. Not after we made an agreement."

Did she order him off her property, as her father, no doubt, would have done? Did she tell him he was an asshole, a bully, a cowardly little man whose grasp on reality was tenuous at best and who didn't know a thing about either herself or her husband, how could he, how could he know a thing? Did she tell him that she'd have no problem at all getting a restraining order slapped on him? Did she say she was going to call 911? Did she so much as tell him that she wasn't up to another scene? Or did she, in fact, beg him to calm down, swearing that she'd do everything in her power to contain the dogs, to quiet them—she'd have the fence moved if she had to, she didn't want to, the fence had been expensive, but she would if she had to—asking him along the way if he was, by chance, a Vietnam War vet, because it seemed to her that he was very reactive, that sudden noise scared him—it does, doesn't it? And when he said that he knew he sometimes overreacted, but no, he wasn't a vet, it wasn't that, it was his childhood, in Newark, it was during the riots, the Blacks, as we called them then, none of this African American stuff, they were Black then and

we called them the Blacks, it was bad back then, forget about it, you
don't even want to know about it, and that, well, he was, it turned out,
a bit of a World War II buff, so he'd learned a thing or two about what-
she-was-talking-about, post-trauma, only then they called it shell-
shocked, no, that wasn't it, that was after the First War, after World
War II they called it battle fatigue, but what am I saying, you're college
educated, you and your husband, both of you, the thing is, it's no crime
to be ignorant, the crime is knowing you're ignorant and not stopping
along the way to learn a thing or two, I don't have to tell you, do I, you
went to college, I can tell.

Which is when she said: "Actually, I'm a professor."

"Like your husband. Runs in the family. Where do you teach, some
place local? No, wait," he said, tapping himself on the forehead like a
clown figure in a sitcom, with exaggerated movements, with movements indicating that all bets were off, it's time for the clown show now,
"I'm guessing you teach at Westchester County. The community college. Am I right?"

"What?"

"I googled you. I googled Don and June Greenstein. Need to know
who the neighbors are. In your cases, it was easy to find out. You popped
right up. June Greenstein, you teach English as a second language.
Good for you, is what I say, people need to learn to speak English."

She was dumbfounded, struck to her core with a combination
of misery and hilarity and a rage so deep that it threatened to swal-
low her up, to turn her to dust, to a pillar of salt, a pogrom, a mini-
Holocaust, only self-inflicted, and acted-out on the lovely wide front
porch that a merchant in Albany named Richard Gerrino had built for
his family in 1922.

"My last name isn't Greenstein," she said. "That's Don's name, not
mine."

"Yeah?"

"Yeah."

"Dames these days," he said with what she recognized was an attempt at lightheartedness.

"Women's lib flipped everything upside down."

"Be that as it may," she said, her voice rising from her throat as if it weren't her voice at all but rather, something a character in a Yiddish novel would say, "I teach literature."

"That so."

"At Harvard."

"Huh?"

"I'm a professor, not of law like Don, and not of English as a second language like the person you googled. I'm a professor of Hebrew literature."

He stared.

"Harvard, huh?" he said.

"It's just that Don and I—well, that's why our home is in the middle, in Connecticut." Their home was just over the border from Westchester, barely Connecticut at all, but he could figure that out later if he had to. "Works for both of us."

"Smart people, you Jews. You know what I always said? If you're sick, if you're ever really sick, get yourself a Jewish doctor."

Fuck you, you dick, she whispered to his departing back, vowing that if he ever set foot on her property again she'd tell him to go fuck himself, call the cops, get a restraining order. But it was too late, she was exhausted now, disgusted with herself, with all her never-satisfied ambitions, all her cries for significance, all her brilliant, brilliant words.

—

By the time Don came back—he'd been running—she was in bed, the dogs on either side of her, with a book she wasn't able to focus on propped open on her lap. "What's wrong?" he said, and when she told him—telling him the whole story, revealing her own petty and stupid lie in its entire stupid falsehood—he said: "He'll google you all over again, probably. And then he'll find out where you really teach."

"I know."

"But I wouldn't worry about it," he said. "First of all, because fuck him. And second of all . . ."

She was hoping he'd say, "You're at Sarah Lawrence, which is impressive enough," but he ran out of words.

"Second of all?"

"There is no second of all," Don said.

"Can I sic the dogs on him?"

"It won't work. They'll just bark. And then they'll cower."

He was right. She began to cry. She cried and cried. She wet the sheets right down to the mattress.

"Should we just sell the house? It isn't worth it, if he's going to be like that."

"But you love this house," Don said. "Why would we sell it? We just got it."

He was right. They just got it. It was hers now—theirs—and no one could take it away, and anyway, the phone was ringing, someone knew they were there. The phone rang and rang and then stopped. She got out of bed, found the bark-collar, went outside, and threw it over the fence into Bob Lesterfield's untidy garden. For a minute or two, she just stood there, waiting to see what would happen, but nothing happened. A bird called. A car passed on the road below. Out on the lake, someone in a motorboat whooped. Why did her father have to die when he did? He'd been seventy-three—not young, but certainly not old, not old enough, anyway, to see the person she'd become, or attend her sons' college graduations, or visit them on the lake. She would have done anything for just one more hour with him, talking about books, about the books he gave her, because somehow, and despite everything, he knew, he'd always known, that she was made of words.

The Second Wife

Adam Singer woke one morning at the usual hour, got out of bed, and died.

It turned out, though, that it was only his soul that had died. But because it had already been dying for some time, Adam didn't notice. What he did notice was that his heart was thumping, his hands and pits were slick with sweat, his throat was dry, and his ears were filled with wind as if he were being hurtled through space. A heart attack, he supposed. A stroke. Something along those lines. He lay face up, breathing.

He'd once wanted to be a doctor—but that had been before he'd flunked out of premed and switched to psychology and then to theater, a major that both his parents and most of his friends found ridiculous. He showed them though. He didn't know how, but he suspected that his success was largely due to his looks: those wide-spaced boiling black eyes, the shaggy brows, the huge smile and twin dimples. It didn't hurt that he was tall, with broad shoulders. All in all, his good looks were an astonishing piece of luck. His mother—now *that* was a tragedy. His father wasn't much better. Between the two of them, they should have produced a child with a head like a boiled potato and body like mashed peas, but instead, they'd produced Adam. And Adam, gorgeous and dimpled with a devilish grin, had grown up to be the star of *Talking Dirt,* now in its fourth season, where he played an escaped convict working as a gardener. To add to the overall perfection, after his first unhappy marriage, he'd married Grace—beautiful, blond, bouncy, talented Grace—and moved from the three-bedroom Spanish-style bungalow near the Santa Monica Freeway where he'd lived unhappily with Caren, to a soaring modern house in Pacific Palisades.

Yes, he was at the top of the world. Too bad it was over. He was so sad about it that he cried.

Feeling the tears trickle down the two sides of his face and dropping onto his neck, he felt a bit silly. His collapse, he now understood, was probably nothing but nerves. Nerves combined with his low blood pressure. He had an audition this afternoon, a big one, a movie, and had been working himself up for days. How desperately he wanted the part!

He got up slowly. He was a bit wobbly, but on the whole, and because he didn't know that his soul had died, he didn't give what he would henceforth call his "episode" much thought. But it did strike him as odd that, when he went downstairs to greet his wife and children, they suddenly appeared to him as ghouls, his wife especially, with her death's head grin, her thick red lipstick and quivering nostrils. The little ones—there were four of them—were milky blue with insubstantiality, with milky blue irises in their skim-milk faces.

Adam himself was the only child of parents who couldn't stand each other and made their shared lives a small but living misery. That little house, in mid-Wilshire, where his widowed mother still lived, with its rooms damp with mediocrity, its walls thick with disappointment. *Of course* he didn't want to replicate that. Who would? He'd always known that about himself—that he was an old-fashioned bring-home-the-bacon kind of guy who wanted nothing more than a big family whom he could take to the beach and to baseball games. The minivan giving way to the Chevy Suburban, the kids growing up, their faces shining out of photo albums and propped in frames on the piano lid in the den. And what, oh *what*, was so wrong, so retro, so sexist about that? But try explaining it to Caren, she'd twist it all up, and before you knew it you'd been cast in the role of misogynistic control freak. How many times had he said, and in these exact words: Go ahead, you're free, do what you want! But Caren hadn't been satisfied. It wasn't enough that he made enough money for the both of them and then some and encouraged her to pursue her dreams. Because her dreams, it turned out, were the opposite of his. She loved quietude, introspection, long walks in nature, hours spent drifting through museums. She liked to work with her hands, to make things: she made quilts, so many of them that she gave them away, and then, as if her need to make things were a tumor growing inside her and taking over larger and larger parts of her being, she started making things out of clay. She took classes. Then she began to photograph things. She developed her photographs and put them on the things she made out of clay. Vessels. Vases. Female forms with enormous bottoms. She travelled to Italy to study how to photograph and how to make things out of clay. And throughout it all—throughout all their ten years together—she adamantly refused to have more than the one disappointing child she seemed so intent on ignoring.

"I don't ignore him," she'd protest. "It's just that I don't indulge him. There's a difference."

"But his grades, Caren! He's barely above average."

"So what? He's eight."

"He has no discipline."

"As I said."

"You need to work with him, build up his confidence, tell him he's smart."

"He'll build up his own confidence himself when he finds something worth doing well. I can't do that for him."

"You don't even help him with his homework."

"And I'm not going to, either."

And on and on it would go like that—around and around and around—while Leo, a boy with the lackadaisical hips of Adam's doughy mother and dour dark face of Caren, remained one of the unseen, the invisible, a shadow among his classmates. While all the other children showed up at school with their homework neatly typed and encased in plastic binders, or with diverse collections of moths and butterflies neatly pinned and labeled on plastic-board, poor old dour-faced Leo handed in cramped reports on wrinkled notebook paper, or a jar of desiccated bee and spider corpses.

"I refuse to be the kind of overbearing, overprotective, pushy mother that cripples her own kids with her own ego-centered unmet needs," Caren would argue, piling more and more references on top of her usual mountain of references, a verbal style that in and of itself made him twitch with impatience. When she was done, he'd counter that he understood that the kid had to figure things out himself, but in the meantime her refusal to conform even a little bit to the prevailing school style turned their kid into a reject.

Then he met Grace. She did his makeup. Their first hurried fuck, behind a standing rack densely hung with overalls, was so spectacular that it was as if his eyeballs had been knocked back in his head and replaced with portals that could take in the great grand glory of God. He felt bad about sneaking around on his wife, but not so bad that he so much as considered stopping. His marriage was over anyhow. Grace was merely the accelerant.

Unlike Grace, who'd grown up among siblings and pets and a whole jumble of visiting cousins, who loved babysitting, and who once wanted to be a kindergarten teacher, Caren didn't particularly like kids at all. She wasn't like other women, or at least not the women he knew. Who didn't like kids? His own mother, as terrible a mother as she'd been, as sour and disappointed, had at least wanted what most other women of her own time had wanted, namely: a husband, a house, a family, and a car. Adam had been an only child only because his mother's health was at risk. Count your blessings, she was told after the miracle that was Adam arrived, and she did until the inevitable misery of life with his father had sunk in, and she'd barely been able to breathe without sending great green gusts of pinched anxiety into the atmosphere.

His father. What a schlump. On the other hand, his mother, such a beggar. How desperately she'd wanted and then demanded not just love but admiration from the husband who was already showing signs of a future that would never open up for him—the too shiny ties, the too well-groomed hair, the smile that seemed rehearsed when in fact it was just a nervous tic. Love he didn't possess—not for himself, not for her, not even for Adam except in dribs and drabs.

Then his father died, doing it in a rather spectacular way, and after the shock of it was over and everything calmed down again, his mother, rather than lighten up, rather than go out and smell the roses and feel the warmth of the sun on her face, dug in, burrowing like a rodent in the bungalow she'd shared with her husband for four decades.

And all the while, the only person who put up with her, who wasn't affected by her moods or dismayed by the stale air inside her cramped house was Caren. Unless, that is, you counted Leo. Leo quite liked his grandmother. He called her Bubbe. Her idea, of course, because not in a million years would Adam have chosen Yiddish over a simple, straightforward "Grandma" or "Nana." His parents' frequent turns into the Yiddishism of their own childhoods in cold, worn-out non-places in the Midwest had irked him. Why had they moved to Southern California if they were so insistent on clinging to their semi-impoverished, light-leached, Yiddish inflected past? Then again, who cared? He didn't. Except, sometimes, when he did, but that was only because a large part of his appeal as an actor was that he could pass as an all-American, star-spangled-bannered, full-blooded, full-throttled, football-playing, beer-drinking ur-goy. He was a cake, made of ingredients put together just so, mixed, whipped, baked, and frosted. And who doesn't love cake?

Caren didn't. When she caught wind of Grace, she didn't even try
to work things out. No tearful trips to the marriage counselor or talks
that went late into the night. No scenes. No threats. Not much of anything, in fact, other than cold, mournful disdain. Had she ever loved
him? She claimed that she did. She claimed that she *still* did. It was
just, she said, that she loved her own soul more.

"Your own soul?" he said. "What are you frigging talking about?"

She stared at him then, staring with those sad doleful eyes of hers.
"Let me remind you that you're the one who's getting off with a teenager," she said.

"She's not a teenager."

"Tell me about it."

"The age gap between my parents was bigger."

"And you see how well that worked out?" Caren answered even
though he hadn't even finished making the point.

"Grace is closer to thirty than twenty."

"I'm impressed," Caren said. "Does your mother know?"

"About Grace?"

"Of course about Grace. What else could I possibly mean?"

"She might," he admitted. How well Caren knew him! But why he'd
gone to his mother before he'd breathed a word of it to anyone else
he himself didn't know. It had seemed like a good idea at the time. To
confess all to his mother, who would understand, and accept him for
all that he was. Which made no sense—not to him, not to Caren, and
certainly not to his mother, who, after he'd finished pouring his heart
out to her, merely said:

"I figured it was something big if you took all the trouble to actually
visit me in person."

"Mom—" he began to protest.

"But I didn't figure on this. I really didn't. Because whatever you
are, I've never known you to be a putz."

"Mother, I came to you for—"

"For what? My blessing? My blessing you don't have. My empathy? I'm not sure you have that either. Understanding? Wisdom? What do I know? Look around. My life—it hasn't added up to much, has it? Not by you. You never come to see me. You never visit. You know who visits? Caren—Caren comes over, we sit, we chat, sometimes we have coffee, she brings the kid, we play a game of Parcheesi or Monopoly—that little devil loves beating his Bubbe, let me tell you, and he's not subtle about it either—and when we say goodbye and she tells me she'll come again before too long I feel happy, and you know why?"

He didn't. He stared at his knees.

"Because when she says that, I know she means it. I know I won't be forgotten. I know she'll call and chat and put the kid on the phone and if he wants to, the three of us, we'll visit the dinosaur museum."

She'd always called the La Brea tar pits the "dinosaur museum," which for some reason made him grind his teeth in rage. Maybe it was the slovenly way she said it, as if she took pleasure in sounding stupid. Or maybe it was just one of the millions of things she'd said to him over the years that landed wrong, leaving its own oily streak. Or maybe, as Caren would say after he'd left her for Grace, he was just a dick.

—

Grace didn't see it that way. Grace said: "The fact of the matter is, your mother is toxic for you. Maybe she doesn't even know it. She probably doesn't. People can be utterly unconscious, completely lacking in self-awareness." Even so, in the early days Grace had very much wanted to be a part of Adam's little family: to be not just his wife, but Leo's stepmother and his mother's daughter-in-law. She'd been so enthusiastic that she quit her job doing makeup to start a blog, *Gratefully Grace*. On it she blogged about her new life with Adam and his family, putting it all out there until, with each succeeding pregnancy, her blog morphed into something bigger, a series with videos that she produced under her own (new) name and sent out into the world like a self-replicating virus: How to step into the role of stepmother. How to step into the role of second wife. How to deal with First Wife. How to merge the roles of career go-getter with home chef. How to keep the bedroom sexy. No blogs about how to deal with the nanny, though. The nanny—whomever it was this month—was never mentioned. Still. Grace not only had an audience but a revenue stream too. Advertising space. Affiliate products. Membership even! She may have started in makeup and hair, but it was she, and not Adam, who had the real gift. How her eyes lit up in front of the camera. How she teased the mic! But in the end none of it mattered. If at first she was wary of Caren, over the years her wariness morphed into a jealousy so all-consuming that there was no place left for Adam at all: the relationship was between his second wife and his first wife. But Caren, that mutt, didn't notice. She stayed in the small bungalow near the Santa Monica Freeway and made things out of clay, feathers, sand, and rope.

"The woman lives to undermine me," Grace said.

"Who? Caren?"

"I told you not to say that name in my presence!"

It was messed up. On the other hand, in six years she'd produced four kids, four lovely slim-hipped and non-dour children who looked like a combination of his dimples and her almond-shaped eyes.

It wasn't until later that day, when Adam was on the set, that he noticed that something was different, better. What should have been a straight-up affair, involving his character's fumbling attempt to hide incriminating documents under a bed of rhododendron, became bigger than that. The lines he delivered were not those of a television actor with a deft touch, but something akin to greatness. So astonishing was his performance that when the scene was completed, the entire cast and crew burst into applause. And he knew then that his gift wasn't small after all, but radiant, and special, and knew, too, that he would nail the audition.

He couldn't wait to get home to tell his wife about how well he'd done. So well, in fact, that the director came right out and told him that he'd blown him away. But as he let himself into the house, Grace was working.

"Or you could have sex instead!" she was saying into the perfect rectangle of light that had long since become her place of worship. "Who says that just because you're a mom you don't still have a right to enjoy sex? It's what got you into this mess to begin with, right? So I say: drop the little ones off at camp or the babysitter, make a date with your husband, or better yet, surprise him by showing up wearing nothing but perfume!" On and on she went. These days, the two of them rarely had any kind of sex at all, including kissing, which wasn't sex, it was kissing. And the children—where were the children? Who knew? Perhaps they were in the rec room.

When he walked in, they didn't even look up from their smartphones for the older two and My First Two-in-Ones for the youngers.

Nor did the nanny—this one, he believed, was Filipina—who was engrossed with something on television. The blur, the blare, he never noticed what the various hired help watched on TV, except this time, he did. She was fixated on an image of Adam himself. Adam as "Thumbs" O'Leary, in one of the early episodes. It didn't make sense that *Talking Dirt* had gone into reruns, only now that he was paying attention he saw that she wasn't watching the television but rather a screen affixed to a projector, itself affixed to a PC. And there he was, his dimples, his square chin.

As he watched the nanny watching him in the personage of "Thumbs" O'Leary, the room caught on fire. One by one each of his children, their nanny, and his own body caught flame, turning a hideous flaking black before disappearing in a plume of ash. As he rose through the ceiling and then up to the second floor, he hovered for a moment to watch his wife's performance: "Ladies, what do you think, that I don't sometimes get the blues? Of course I do! What with all the hats I wear—mother, stepmother, career counselor, bread baker, gardener, chauffeur, lover, daughter-in-law, daughter, and wife! Sometimes I get so dizzy all I want to do is put on a comfy pair of sweats and do nothing all day but eat chocolate."

But once again he wasn't dead at all, but rather, as he blinked himself awake, standing in a trance in the first-floor rec room of his own home.

—

It wasn't until after the children were in bed and he was alone eating dinner with Grace that the call came through, on his cell phone. Not too many people had his cell phone number; as an actor he had to be careful about giving it out. It was a woman's voice on the phone, saying something about his mother. His mother had had a fall. She was at Cedars-Sinai: internal bleeding, loss of consciousness.

"I'm on my way," he said.

"You're on your way where?" Grace said.

"My mother's at the hospital. She's had an accident."

"Your mother," she said. "What kind of accident?"

"I don't know."

"It's probably nothing."

"I have to go anyway."

"I'll go with you."

"It's not necessary."

"Don't you want me?"

"Whatever you want," he said.

They started out for the hospital but got stopped for more than an hour by an accident on 101, and when at last they began to move, they moved at a crawl. When they arrived, they found Adam's mother hooked up to a machine and barely breathing, her eyes closed and her face bruised. Caren was sitting by the window, reading. Her hair, he noticed, was beginning to frost at the edges, a tracing of gray.

"What is *she* doing here?" Grace said.

"Where's Leo?" Adam said.

"Leo's at home."

"You left him at home?"

"He's fifteen. A sophomore in high school."

"No he's not."

"Hate to break it to you."

Stupid—a stupid stupid thing to say. Of course Leo was in high school. He knew that. Leo spent every other weekend at his father's house in Pacific Palisades. His feet had become enormous.

"What happened to Mom?" Adam now said. "I don't understand."

"She jumped off a bridge."

"What?"

"The overpass at Hollywood Boulevard." Caren said it with little more intonation than if she were ordering Chinese. "Landed in the bed of a pickup truck. That's why she survived. The driver, he watched the whole thing happen, called 911. And now, as you see—"

He did see. His poor mother, bloated, bruised, her skin gone yellow on the outskirts of the bruises, with cracks of lurid red blood where her skin had split. She was stitched together, moored, exhausted, and bitterly disappointed. And now this—awful misadventure. The one daring thing she'd ever attempted, and it too was a failure.

"I think she may have missed your father more than she let on," Caren said.

Adam's father had died years before when he drove over a cliff. But instead of smashing against the rocks and cacti, his car landed in a swimming pool. Adam's father, dressed in swimming trunks and an IDF T-shirt, was trapped at the wheel. By the time they extracted him, he was the same color as the water. Was it suicide? There was no note. Had he been under the influence? Toxicity reports came back negative. His death made the news cycle all the same.

In an apparent accident, father of actor Adam Singer, star of ABC's popular *Talking Dirt*, was found in the early hours of . . .

It had been terrible: a photographer from *People* magazine had taken pictures of him and his then pregnant second wife as they emerged from the limousine that had taken them from the funeral home to the cemetery. Another had awaited him on his doorstep. If his mother actually died they'd have a field day. He became nauseous just thinking about it.

No one wanted an actor associated with suicide at top or even second billing, and as he scrolled through the various outcomes that might happen, including (most assuredly) not being offered the part he'd just auditioned for, he knew with a clarity born of no longer having a soul that no matter what, Grace would spin the occasion into gold. He went home. He prayed that his mother would recover. The next day, he went back to the hospital and held her hand.

—

His mother died of her injuries anyway, and sure enough, after the seven days of shiva, Grace became so animated that she actually appeared before him as an animated version of herself, all clean lines and exaggerated features as she talked into her computer screen about the tragedy of her dear mother-in-law's sad end, because death comes to all of us, but suicide is something that has to be dealt with on its own terms, as it slowly unfolds in all its horrors . . .

But before that, and well before she'd launched herself into the web stratosphere and he got the role that would lead to the next role that would lead to his being not only a household name but a face so familiar that he was recognized wherever he went, Grace stood next to him by his mother's bedside at Cedars-Sinai, crying: "Dear God, don't let her die!"

Acknowledgments

Some stories in the collection have been previously published in *Commentary*, *The Gettysburg Review*, *Tikkun*, *Image*, *Nimrod*, *The Antioch Review*, *Another Chicago Magazine*, *Michigan Quarterly Review*, and *The Other Journal*.

The author would like to thank Kris Fischer, Sandi Wisenberg, Garnett Kilberg-Cohen, and the entire excellent crew at the University of Wisconsin Press, with special thanks to Dennis Lloyd. To my children and husband: thank you for always being on my team.